ANTI HERO

Skye Warren

Nate Gaines knows he's no hero. After losing his team in a fiery betrayal, he left the army. Now he works for cold hard cash.

And the girl he loves? She's better off without him.

Until her story makes her a target.

Then he'll protect her. He'll kill for her. He just won't let himself fall for her again. That would be dangerous, for both of them.

WARNING: Contains an inked military man, a plucky reporter on a mission, and explosive chemistry!

FOREWORD

Anti Hero is action-packed, with plenty of explosive chemistry! If you love swoonworthy alpha military heroes, you don't want to miss Liam North from OVERTURE…

Liam North got custody of the violin prodigy six years ago. She's all grown up now, but he still treats her like a child. No matter how much he wants her.

"Swoon-worthy, forbidden, and sexy, Liam North is my new obsession."

– New York Times bestselling author
Claire Contreras

CHAPTER ONE

THE CEILING FAN turned above her, barely moving the hot summer air. Sweat dampened her nightgown, but she didn't push the comforter off. Even the daylight touching her skin was too much. She wanted to be hidden, in the dark. That was how she'd been living for the past month.

Heavy footsteps came up the stairs, too heavy to be her grandmother. *Diego.*

She kept her gaze on the ceiling even when the door opened.

Silence. Then a sigh. The chair beside her bed creaked.

"Abuela says you aren't eating," Diego said.

Without looking she could envision her brother's skin, darker than hers from hours spent outside smoking pot and drinking with his friends. His long lashes were too pretty for a boy. He got them from their mother. His cold gray eyes made up the difference. Those came from their father.

Tucked into his waistband would be the red bandanna that marked his gang's color. Outside the house he wore it bigger, wrapped around his forehead or neck. Moving it down was supposed to make him more like her brother, but it didn't work.

"Not hungry."

"She's making your favorite. Posole."

She already knew that because the scent of spices filled the house. Maybe a month ago she would have been in the kitchen, writing in her journal at the dining room table while her mouth watered. Now her stomach felt like lead, still and solid. It didn't want any food. And she didn't want her brother.

"Go away."

Another sigh. She glanced over and saw that he'd put his fingers together, his face turned sideways. She could study his hard features and wonder when he'd gotten that scar at his eyebrow. His face was so familiar to her, but different too.

His eyes squinted, and for a moment she thought he might actually mention *it*. The thing they didn't talk about. The reason she was cooking herself beneath the covers. The moment he'd chosen his gang over his family. No, that wasn't right. He'd chosen the gang over his family the moment he'd worn that red bandanna.

Instead he said, "Do you remember that flood?"

Back when they'd been living closer to the border, a flood had dropped millions of gallons of rain on the small south Texas town. Water had crawled up the sloped lawns, past the weeds and concrete saints. Then it crept inside the houses, turning the thin carpets to sludge. Higher and higher, until Sofia and her family had taken refuge on their patched roof, homemade quilts wrapped around them and the contents of their pantry in plastic bags beside them.

Most days Daddy had come back from the factory too exhausted, too angry to do anything but eat the plate Mama made for him and go to sleep. That was better than the days he came home drunk. Then his anger came out in shouts and fists.

The flood had transformed him, if only for a week.

As he looked at them huddled together with whatever they could carry, fear ripe in his eyes, he'd seemed to grow taller. A few houses down the neighbor had a small boat he set traps with. The engine had broken, but they used slats of broken fence as oars to scout the neighborhood, making sure everyone had gotten out, that they had fresh water and enough food to last until authorities could evacuate them.

They all had sunburns when they finally got in the boat to meet the helicopter that had landed a mile away.

Daddy's hands had been ripped apart, bloodied, filled with splinters.

Sofia didn't want to remember that, didn't want to remember the time before the crash, when her parents were still alive. She didn't want to remember huddling with her big brother, believing he'd keep her safe.

She didn't want to remember anything.

But the fear she felt ripped through the numb veil that had protected her. There was something else there too. Pride. "The puppy."

Diego made a rough sound. "The damned puppy. How did it even swim that long?"

She didn't bother to shrug. The second day her father had spotted a puppy paddling through the window, fur slicked to his body, movements slow. They had guessed he managed to sit on some of the furniture for a while, so he hadn't been swimming nonstop. But he didn't know how to get out.

Afraid breaking the window would scare him

away, or hurt him, their father had swam through the murky water to the back door, then through the house, past anchorless sofas and kitchen tables, soggy picture frames and broken glass, to pull the puppy out.

The puppy had come to stay on the roof with them for the next two days, living on cheese crackers and peanut butter. The newspapers had called her dad a hero.

"You should eat," Diego said, glancing at her. She had hardly looked in the mirror. What would he see? Her split lip. Bruises. Bloodshot eyes from lack of sleep.

He looked back at his hands.

They were large hands, like her father's. Not bloodied and splintered.

He hadn't been a hero.

CHAPTER TWO

Present day

SOFIA HUNG UP from another fruitless phone call, another dead end. She rubbed her eyes, so tired of hitting her head against the nearly impenetrable wall named Senator Stephen Moreland. His finances were tied up so tight she couldn't even see a crack. Assuming there was anything to find.

She knew there was.

She'd been researching political finance since she started at the *Daily* two years ago. She had interned under a reporter who went to the *Washington Post*. And the number of secrets on this campaign was unprecedented.

He was dirty. She just had to prove it.

"That bad, huh?" Remy plopped down in her chair with a sympathetic expression. As a fellow reporter, she knew how much it sucked coming up empty.

Their desks faced each other, so when she

wasn't looking at her monitor, she saw Remy, who sported a new look every week. Today her sandy-blonde hair was tied in an intricate braid, with colorful strands of hemp sewn through. Her army-green raglan shirt read *Department of Redundancy Department.*

Sofia tossed her phone onto her cluttered desk. "That was the third aide who never knew Moreland owned property in Austin."

"You think he's telling the truth?"

She drummed her fingers on the desk. "Probably."

The aide had asked her out for coffee twice, once when she'd cornered him at a taco stand and again on the call just now. If he'd had any information to give, he would have used it as bait. As desperate as she was, she probably would have taken it.

Moreland had disclosed his campaign finances by the book. At least some of his personal property was public knowledge—the private jet, the hotel in Boston. It was here in Texas, near the southern border of the country, that his interests got murkier.

There was more money, *secret* money, and she was determined to find it.

Sofia tapped her pen. "I need to find out what

goes on during those trips. That's where he's vulnerable. I'm tempted to drive over there and look around."

The frequent trips to Mexico under the guise of drug control or anti-trafficking reform were bizarre. What was he going to do, have a thoughtful conversation with drug lords and convince them to stop? There were no press ops of him shaking hands with leaders or smiling at children on these trips, either. Everything was hush-hush.

Remy frowned. "You know I love your determination, sweetheart. That's what makes you a great reporter. Best one I know. But this guy…he's dangerous."

"This coming from the girl who meets her sources on the streets," she said absently, her mind focused on the files Rick had uploaded. Budget cuts meant they'd lost most of their support staff, including the last archivist who loved to comb old newspapers.

Instead she had resorted to free labor—an intern who worked at the university's paper. She e-mailed him an assignment. He uploaded the files into the *Daily*'s servers via VPN.

Scooting forward in her chair, she found the files in the network folder and dragged them onto her desktop, sighing when she saw they'd take ten minutes to copy over. The tech infrastructure here was outdated, old-school. Forget the cloud; they had servers the size of entire rooms in the basement.

She'd take the files home, look them over tonight with a cup of instant noodles.

Was this what her social life had come to?

"I'm serious," Remy said. "It's one thing to do a report on the state of his campaign finances. It's another to go snooping around in his private life."

Except this article would actually be about campaign finance, the *true* state of his campaign finance, including kickbacks or unsavory connections. And Sofia had spent too much of her life trembling, running. Hiding. She wouldn't hide this time.

Nate had taught her to be strong, even though he wouldn't believe it.

God, Nate. That slight smile, the ever-present scruff. The colorful ink covering his muscled body. And of course, the laid-back Southern-boy charm. They had been together for three glorious months before everything had imploded.

She might have believed his *don't give a fuck* attitude if she hadn't lain naked next to him, draped over his chest while she talked about the injustices she covered at work. His heart had raced, whole body tense and ready for combat. He cared, all right. He just didn't want to.

Beside her laptop, her cell phone flashed a message to the screen. A voice mail had been left. Cell reception was spotty in these old buildings. It hadn't even rung.

Excitement beat in her chest as she checked the phone number.

Not Nate. Of course not.

She tried not to be disappointed.

While Remy picked up a bomb-shaped stress ball from her desk, Sofia listened to the message. Static sounded in her ear, and she winced. Her mood didn't improve as she heard the stuttering voice of her landlord, Ernie. It sounded like he got even worse reception than she did. Only a few words pierced the noise: "When are you coming…right away…"

The hair on the back of her neck prickled. She called him back, but it went straight to his voice mail.

"That was weird."

Remy missed the catch, and the stress ball rolled beneath the heavy metal desk against the wall. Her gaze sharpened. "Who was that?"

"My landlord."

"Panty-smelling guy?"

"I wish you wouldn't call him that," she muttered.

"Oh come on, he accidentally takes your laundry out of the dryer, not noticing the lacy panties that don't belong to him?"

Yeah, that had been awkward. Sofia maintained that nothing inappropriate had happened—but she'd still thrown the entire load of laundry away when he'd returned it.

"I think he wants me to come back to the apartment."

"Booty call," Remy said.

She made a face. "Don't be like that. He's never called me at work before. I hope everything's okay."

"Right, I'm sure there's a plumbing emergency." Remy pitched her voice high. "Sofia, my faucet was so lonely without you. Won't you unclog it for me?"

Sofia chucked a pen in her friend's direction. It bounced off a two-year-old calendar on the wall and clattered to the floor. The file transfer was only at eighty-two percent, so she'd have to wait another minute at least.

Remy just laughed. "You're the one living with him."

"I live above him, not with him. And I love my apartment. It has a sunroom, and I can afford the rent. If he comes on to me…again…I'll just shut him down."

"That's sexual harassment."

Eighty-nine percent. "The only one sexually harassing me right now is you."

"Whatever, he's a creep."

"He's not a creep. He's just…"

What was he? He had this way of cringing with every word he spoke, as if he was afraid of a rebuke at any moment. His gaze tripped over every corner of the room, unable to meet hers.

Okay, he was a creep.

But a nice one, and Sofia wasn't afraid of him. Maybe she felt a little bad for him. And she *really* liked her apartment.

"I can deal with him," she finished.

Remy rolled her eyes and turned back to her monitor.

Sofia didn't blame her friend for her concern. Remy worked the crime beat, where she spoke to battered women and victimized runaways every day. She expected the worst from people.

When they went out for girl's night, Remy didn't just keep an eye on their drinks, she guarded everyone's, on the lookout for sneaky hands and dissolving pills. And God save the man who tried to take home a wasted girl on Remy's watch. She was Austin's own warrior princess.

How long had it been since they'd gone out? Too long. They sat across from each other all day at work, then went home and worked some more. Not exactly glamorous, but it was hard to get excited about the club scene. Had she ever been? The frat boys who called her *senorita* as if it was so clever.

Her black hair and tanned skin weren't even rare. On Austin's east side, every girl looked like her, but she didn't belong there either. There she was a commodity, to be sold and traded. She tried to forget those times.

A shiver ran down her spine, memories like a cold finger.

She'd tried to hide her past from Nate, but he was smart. He'd figured out the gist when she'd flinched away from his touch. And then he'd been careful with her. An incredibly masculine man, powerful, rugged—and he'd touched her with absolute gentleness. Soothed her until she learned how to find pleasure in his arms, found release in his roughness.

She wasn't supposed to think about Nate.

The folder blinked on her laptop screen. The

file transfer was complete.

She shut the laptop and tucked it into its bag. "Do you think we should go out more?"

Remy stared at her blankly. "Out where?"

"I don't know. To have fun."

"You know what would be fun? Not poking a shady politician and risking your neck."

"Very funny." Sofia stood and stretched. "You could come hang out at my place and look at these articles with me."

Remy's gaze flicked toward their editor's office. "Not tonight."

Curiosity tugged at her. "Is Andre giving you a hard time?"

He was the quintessential newspaper editor, which meant he yelled a lot about deadlines and copyedits and budget cuts. But he was passionate about the truth. He was also one of the few people who knew about her suspicions of Moreland, besides Remy.

Remy's smile felt forced. "Nothing I can't handle."

Sofia would let it go for now, but she made a mental note to take Remy out soon for drinks. Maybe getting hit on by rowdy drunk guys would do them both good. They could run a competition for who got the cheesiest pickup line.

She swung her laptop bag over her shoulder and headed to Andre's door.

He looked up from his computer, though his fingers continued typing for another beat. His chestnut hair was askew, shirtsleeves rolled up, eyes bloodshot—so, business as usual.

"What's up, Reyes?"

"Is it okay if I cut out early? Something's up with my apartment."

"No problem at all. Just stay late the next five nights and we'll call it even."

"I wish you were joking."

"Me too," he said, waving her away. "Now go see what sunlight looks like and report back tomorrow."

With a wry smile, she left the office. All editors were hard-asses. She figured that was part of the job description. But now that she thought about it, he had been on Remy's case more than usual lately. Maybe there was something going on between them. Wouldn't that be scandalous? Definitely girl's night. She'd get answers then.

The *Daily*'s offices took up the top floor of the old, three-story building. Escalators brought her to the ground floor, which was bustling at the height of the afternoon. The sunlight blinded her, burning her eyes.

Her sunglasses were probably on her desk. She hesitated, debating whether to run upstairs and get them. The bus was already idling on the opposite street corner. At any minute, the driver would shut the door and pull away from the curb. Her apartment was only a twenty-minute walk, not much for the pedestrian-friendly city, but her laptop bag cut into her shoulder. She wanted that bus.

Damn it. She dashed to the corner. A heavy stream of pedestrians filled the sidewalk, but she darted through, jogging the last few feet as the crosswalk sign flipped to the white hand.

Through the large, reflective windows, she saw the bus driver reach for the door lever. Swearing under her breath, she raised her hand to grab his attention. Too late. The doors swung shut, and the bus started forward with a high-pitched whine.

She stopped, watching the orange stripe along the bus streak across her vision and disappear. Damn. Adjusting the strap of her bag so it mashed her shoulder at another angle, she turned toward home, ready to walk.

A large boom rocked the earth.

She tripped from the shock, crashing against the white-hot pavement. For a moment, she lay there stunned. Had she been hit by a car? In degrees, her hearing returned, bringing with it the shouts and screams of people as bewildered as her. She levered herself up, lurching unsteadily as she looked back and found the source of the blast.

The bottom right corner of the *Daily*'s building was gone, unveiling burnt metal servers that opaque windows and concrete cornices had once blocked from view. Melted metal and exposed rubble formed a grotesque sculpture.

Andre. Remy.

She ran toward the building, the laptop bag flapping painfully against her hip. Yanking it off her neck, she let it fall onto the sidewalk and kept running.

People were fleeing from the building, a current too strong to fight through. From ten feet away, she stood, jostled by terrified survivors exiting the building and horrified to realize there was nothing she could do. There was a human wall blocking her entrance, and even if she could get past it, what then? The sounds of sirens in the air spurred her to action. Farther down, a side door opened, and a handful of shock-blind people tumbled out. She ran for it, yanking open the metal door.

Someone caught her arm and pulled her back.

"You can't go in there."

"My friends." She struggled with him, tugging at her arm until he caught her up in a binding bear hug. He was a stranger to her. Barely human—just a flash of wide brown eyes and the white squiggly letters of a *Keep Austin Weird* shirt, but she melted against him for a second as he squeezed her tight. He was only trying to keep her safe. They were both helpless here, fallen leaves buffeted by the wind and snagged on each other for a moment's consolation.

She pushed back with a hoarse, angry cry. Anger toward the nameless, faceless people who'd done this, because she didn't believe for a second that an explosion in Austin's newspaper was an accident. Anger at herself for not being able to help. And anger at her terrible, selfish relief. *I was almost inside. Almost.*

Two police cars screeched their way to a stop in front of the building. The cops began forcing everyone back, away from the building. Like an animal to slaughter, she bumped against the people around her but ultimately moved where directed. Everyone was talking—to their neighbor, to themselves—but it all filtered through the sludge that was her brain.

She was trembling, inside and out, chilled in

places she'd barely been aware of. Only a few seconds had passed, minutes maybe, but everything had changed. She was hypersensitive now, wincing from a slight breeze and stumbling over every crack in the sidewalk tiles.

If she hadn't gotten the phone call, if Andre hadn't told her to go, she would be crushed beneath rubble, burning, dying… Oh God, her friends. It looked like the blast had happened in the data center—maybe a loose wire had triggered the explosion. Although she suspected something more sinister.

She didn't know the extent of the damage, couldn't know how the structure of the old building would hold up. Andre might want her to take pictures. To pull out her camera, her laptop, anything, and start recording. Give the *Daily* the scoop on its own downfall.

She couldn't do that, not even for Andre, even though he deserved her loyalty, because one thought stayed with her: she could be dead right now.

And she couldn't shake the feeling that she might still be in danger.

In this business, twenty-four years old was more than old enough to be jaded—and suspicious. There were a million reasons to explain why the *Daily*'s offices were just blown to bits, hundreds of high-profile stories, so many of her colleagues inside. It probably had nothing to do with her or her story, but it might.

Don't make assumptions. She still held out hope that her friends would be fine, that the firemen piling out of trucks would pull them from harm. Her stomach turned over. She couldn't help them now, whether they were injured, in the capable hands of the doctors. This would be her promise to Andre, to fulfill her obligation to her story.

Breaking free of the pack, she backtracked to where her messenger bag lay askew on the sidewalk. The laptop had slid out, exposed, but the blast must have distracted any would-be thief from picking it up and walking away with it. If she hung around until the cops sorted everything out, her electronics would be confiscated. She would be held and questioned. It would all take months to sort out, if ever, giving Moreland time to cover any tracks that were left.

Wait, she didn't know that Moreland was responsible for this. Another hunch, useless without evidence or corroboration. Slinging the bag over her shoulder, she slipped around the corner. She needed to regroup. To catch her breath. At the next corner, another bus lurched forward, preparing to enter the stream of traffic. She ran right in front of it, waving wildly at the driver, who frowned and jerked the bus to a halt.

She pounded on the door. After a moment's hesitation, the heavyset driver swung the lever.

"We're not taking on any more passengers," he said. "There's been an incident."

An incident. That was one word for it.

"Please. I just need to go a few blocks. I need to get home."

After a brief pause, he nodded. She hopped up the tall steps and fell into the first empty seat as the bus lurched forward. The seats were mostly empty. Only an older woman in one of the rows and a young man with spiky hair in the backseat. Neither seemed interested in her or upset at all. They probably didn't even know about the explosion yet.

Her entire axis had shifted, but these people had only heard thunder.

She studied the colorful route lines on the placards above the seats. This wasn't her usual route, so it was going to take her farther away before circling back near her apartment. Her hands trembled as she smoothed her black pencil skirt. Her white button-down shirt and patent pumps were a little more formal than what Remy or the other guys at the office wore, but Sofia had always had a thing about professionalism. Ambition, Nate had called it, and it hadn't been a compliment.

She'd missed him over the past few months, but right now it felt deeper, sharper, as if a scab had been ripped off, her old wounds open and raw. She could have been dead, never to see him again, never to hear his voice.

Fumbling in the pockets of the bag, she pulled out her cell phone. His number was still there. She'd never brought herself to deleting it.

The phone rang and rang.

"Pick up," she muttered. "Where are you, Nate?"

She was sure she'd hit voice mail and even thought she heard the little click as it transferred, but then his voice came on the line, as rough and deep as it was in her dreams.

"Sofia?"

"Nate," she breathed. Just hearing his voice warmed her, and she was so very cold.

"Why are you calling?"

Abrupt, maybe even annoyed. Even that couldn't dispel the comfort she took from him. Though it did remind her that they hadn't parted on good terms four months ago. Why was she calling? *Because I almost died. Because you would have been my last thought.*

"I missed you," she said.

He made a rough sound. "You were the one who told me to take a hike."

She hadn't meant it that way. They'd argued about his job, about hers. He'd wanted her to step back, stop taking everything so seriously, and she'd wanted him to start giving a damn. She'd wanted him to stop hiding. Except now he'd removed himself from her life, so far hidden she'd probably never see him again. She'd spent the last four months pretending it was for the best.

"I shouldn't have said what I did. I don't...I don't know what happened to you over there." In Afghanistan or wherever other need-to-know places he'd been. "I can't fix it, Nate. I thought I could, but I can't."

She was stripped bare, the words tumbling forth before she'd had time to analyze them. They were an apology, a confession, and a plea all wrapped into one. Considering what had just happened, this wasn't the most important thing to talk about. Then again, maybe it was. All the things she couldn't say before. Last words to a man she'd loved. The man she still loved.

There was a rustling sound, and she imagined him pushing aside papers on his desk, maybe running his fingers through his hair.

"It was wrong of me to expect you to fix it," he said. "I think I'm just too broken for a relationship. You deserve better, anyway."

She almost laughed. Something caught in her throat, but she was afraid it was a sob instead. Well, what had she expected, calling him after something like that? It was like drunk dialing, only instead of liquor, she was hopped up on fear.

"Okay," she said. "Okay."

"Sofia?" His voice had a new edge. "Is something going on?"

He would hear about the explosion on the news. Would he have worried about her? Yes. She knew that with certainty. They'd had their share of problems, but when he'd looked into her eyes, when he'd been buried deep inside her body and soul, she'd never doubted how much he cared. At least now that she'd called, he wouldn't have to worry.

"I just wanted to hear your voice," she said.

He was quiet, and when he spoke, his voice had gone husky. "I missed you too, Sofia."

Tears sprang to her eyes. She'd wasted the past few months, so anxious about the future that she'd lost the present. Now it was too late. She couldn't involve him in this, whatever it was.

He was Special Forces, whispered a traitorous voice in her mind. And a private investigator now. He had access to resources. Hell, he *was* a resource. But this was dangerous—obviously, considering what had just happened—and she couldn't live with herself if she got him hurt. Besides, he'd made his disdain for her causes very clear. She was on her own.

"I'll see you around," she forced out. "Take care."

"Wait. Sofia—"

She hung up, shutting her eyes against the impulse to call him back, to tell him everything and beg for his help. He was probably cursing her at the other end. *Ring and run,* that was what she'd just done. Starting something she couldn't finish. But she couldn't regret it. It had been really nice to hear his voice.

I've missed you too, Sofia, and the way he spoke her name reminded her of a hundred summer nights, his raw voice repeating it with every thrust, *Sofia, Sofia, Sofia.* They'd been wild and unstoppable then, with nothing covering their bodies but sweat and the scent of sex. He'd worshipped her, and she'd soaked up his feral passion, and everything had been wonderful and perfect until it wasn't anymore.

This bus route circled half of downtown before stopping a block from her apartment building. There was no sidewalk here, just a smooth black gravel street that faded into the grassy ditch on either side. She walked the uneven edge of the pavement, trying to formulate a plan in her head.

A shower sounded tempting. The explosion hadn't touched her, but she felt tainted—dirty. Hot, scalding water sounded like heaven right about now. She'd make it quick, then load up her laptop and check her usual sources for news about the explosion. See if some terrorist group had claimed the attack. It would almost be a relief if someone did, because then she would know. But if the attacker was still unknown, she could look for connections, see if anything led back to Moreland. And if it did? It would mean a solid lead for her story and the sickening confirmation that her friends' injuries—maybe even their deaths—were on her hands.

The houses in this neighborhood were small, three and four bedrooms crammed into a thousand square feet. She'd toured a few of them when they came up for rent, but they cost five times what she paid. Her apartment building only had three units. The bottom floor was occupied by Ernie, who'd inherited the building from his parents. She rented one of the top-floor units, and the other one had been empty since the bachelor had gotten married and bought a house in Round Rock.

The whole thing felt surreal. The day was bright, warm with a slight breeze. A few houses down, a flag hanging by the front door waved in the wind. So goddamned normal, just like this morning, right before the explosion.

She stepped in the small foyer, which contained the main stairwell for the units. Ernie's door was off to the right. So often it opened right as she started up the stairs, and she had to conclude that he watched for her out the window. But today it was already open, revealing the small table in his foyer piled high with mail. Then she remembered the phone call, the one that might have saved her life, even if that had been unintentional. For that reason alone, she should be nicer to Ernie, but she wasn't sure she had the energy to deal with him after what had happened. Still, he'd called for some reason.

Rapping on the door, she tilted her head to see inside. "Ernie? You there?"

Her laptop was calling her name, those files that might somehow explain what had happened this morning. And when Ernie got on a roll, he could spend twenty minutes telling her about his day before she could extricate herself.

Something kept her from going upstairs. A sense of urgency in his voice on the phone. The strangeness of his door being left open like this. Or maybe those were excuses and what she really needed was human contact, validation that she was really alive.

As she nudged the door open and tentatively stepped inside, the irony assailed her. She and Remy had accused him of practically stalking her, but here she was entering his home uninvited. The reminder of Remy sent a fresh slice of pain through her belly.

She peeked into the living room, recognizing the brown leather couches, the large-screen TV from the few times she'd been here before. "Ernie?"

No sign of him.

Damn. Well, she'd tried, and she wasn't comfortable snooping any farther into his apartment. She turned to leave when something caught her eye. Through the kitchen door, she saw a shoe. An old Converse sneaker that she'd seen plenty of times on Ernie's feet. Only this time, it was pointing up.

Dread snaked down her spine. On lead feet, she crossed the small dining room. Ernie was lying on the kitchen floor, his eyes closed and a dark stain spread across his gray T-shirt.

A small cry escaped her as she knelt to check his pulse. Nothing. She fumbled for her phone, about to dial 9-1-1 when she heard the creak. She stilled, frozen with horror. Then another one, this one directly above her. Someone was inside her apartment.

Chapter Three

NATHANIEL GAINES RUBBED the two-day-old scruff he hadn't realized he'd accumulated. This client e-mail was killing him. He'd never been one for diplomacy, but his filter seemed to be getting worse. Certainly, he couldn't write what was in his head:

I'm sorry your wife is cheating on you with her personal trainer. And hairstylist. I'm sorry you bust your ass at work while she shows the tits you bought her to other men. I'm sorry that, from what I can tell, you're a coldhearted bastard, which is why she looks elsewhere for a little affection. And most of all, I'm sorry I picked the lamest job I could find and still use my godforsaken training, but it turns out that private detectives are really just the worst marriage counselors in the world.

Maybe he should carry business cards for a divorce lawyer. Or maybe he should lie and keep them blissfully unaware, if he gave a damn about his clients. Luckily, he didn't give a damn about much. Joining the military had hardened him. Leaving had turned him to fucking stone.

Except when it came to Sofia. He couldn't lie to himself about her.

He really fucking cared about her. And that phone call. What was that about? As he'd so rudely pointed out, she'd been the one to break things off.

Nah, that was bullshit. The truth was, she'd pushed him, wanting more, wanting things he could barely name, much less deliver, and he'd let her walk, because that's what he did. The soldier, who put his work before his own fucking life.

He had no business messing with Sofia; he couldn't promise her the future she deserved, couldn't even be honest with her about where he spent his nights. But she'd called and he was helpless to resist the pull. If she wanted to start things up again...hell, to hook up for just a night...he'd be at her front door with fucking bells on.

Dishonorable, but the God's honest truth.

Of course, she hadn't asked him out or propositioned him. *I'll see you around,* she'd said. And her voice had been strange. He couldn't put his finger on how she'd sounded.

Nervous, maybe? Shaky.

Scared.

He didn't like it. He liked the confident Sofia, the one who went down on him with a wicked smile, who called his bullshit when she thought he should care more. He'd only seen the scared Sofia a few times before, when he first touched her. When she thought he would hurt her.

Fuck.

The thought of swinging by to check on her wouldn't let him go. He'd done a lot of stupid shit in his life; he really didn't want to add stalking his ex to the list. Still, he could just drive by. He wouldn't have to actually talk to her. Make sure she was okay, that no asshole other than him was hassling her.

He'd heard the ding of the Austin Metro service in the background. Why was she on the bus at this time of day? The whole time they'd been together, she'd put in long hours at the paper, then come home and worked some more. At first it had been fine. A workaholic—convenient, because she didn't question his crazy hours.

As they'd grown closer, they'd made up for the long hours at work by staying up late together, sweating and panting and talking until the sky turned pale blue. But she kept wanting him to give a fuck, and he'd lost all his fucks in that godforsaken desert, so here they were.

It wouldn't be stalking. Okay, it would be, but he was officially a private detective, after all. That was basically a professional stalker. His secret job, his *real* profession, wasn't much better.

He'd just see if she'd made it home okay.

If they started talking and she invited him inside…hey, it could happen. Showing up empty-handed might be awkward. Maybe he could pick up flowers on the way.

Goddamn it.

This was exactly what he was trying to avoid. This desperate yearning ache that always left him cold and disappointed and, once upon a time, laid up in the hospital with a blasted kneecap. Okay, so the last part wasn't likely to happen with Sofia, but it illustrated the point. He'd once thought he was invincible, that if he believed and fought and cared enough that the world would bend to his will. All that had gotten him was twelve months of physical training before he could walk again and a Dear John discharge letter from the army. A soldier wasn't much use with a bum knee. *Thanks for your service, now get lost.*

He leaned back in his chair, running his hand through his hair. Damn, it was long. When had that happened? Shaggy and curling up at his shirt collar. He must look like a bastard. All the more reason Sofia would tell him to take a hike. But he was definitely going to see her.

Before leaving the office, he loaded up his Sig. He didn't usually carry it during his day job and never on a freaking date. There was really no good reason to now, except for that tremor in Sofia's voice that he just couldn't shake.

Nate had known he wasn't good company for a woman when he got back. He was too fucked up, both mind and body. But then he'd seen Sofia. One look at the determination in her gorgeous brown eyes and he'd been gone.

Even seeing her skittish about his size, his touch hadn't turned him away. From somewhere deep he'd found the strength to be gentle, to go slow with her. He had earned her trust. She deserved that much from him.

Usually it was the guy who got weird about commitment, but in this case, she'd gotten nervous. Wondering whether they had a future, wondering if a guy like him even had a future. He didn't blame her. No, he knew it was for the best when she walked away.

Except now she had called him, sounding small, sounding scared. He would go to her and destroy anyone who had made her feel that way.

He just wasn't sure he could let her go a second time.

Chapter Four

Ten years ago

SOFIA PRESSED HER hand over her mouth, fighting the nausea that came only at night. For weeks the numbness had cocooned her, and she hadn't known to be grateful. Little by little, the real world had poked holes in her paper walls.

First a strange pang in her stomach she finally realized was hunger.

Then the suffocating heat of her clothes, her blankets, the scalding showers.

Pain came last. She longed for the numbness to return, but she couldn't make it. Abuela was glad that she was eating again and leaving her room. But she didn't know about the pain.

One night Abuela had found her throwing up in the middle of the night, so Sofia had had to put up with more doctor exams. She wasn't pregnant, thank God. Hadn't picked up any diseases, either. She supposed she should be grateful, but she couldn't be, not as she retched into a bowl, knowing she'd already vomited all of it for the night.

The TV helped distract her, late-night shows that numbed her mind.

Books where girls had evil twins and handsome teachers.

Right now she had none of that, the lights off, a ceramic bowl clutched in her shaking hands.

Scuffs and scratching noises from the door startled her. She held the bowl harder, until her knuckles hurt, listening. What if they had come back? They would eventually. Her stomach clenched. Of course they would. It would never be over.

There was no place to hide in the house. They would find her bedroom easy. Break the flimsy lock.

Abuela was a heavy sleeper, and anyway, she couldn't protect her.

She grabbed her quilt and scooted to the floor, in the two-foot space between the Goodwill couch and the wall. All she had was her bowl as a shield, eyes wide in the familiar room.

The door swung open, throwing moonlight across the vinyl floor. A long shadow drew closer. *No no no.* Saying no didn't help. Tears leaked out of her eyes.

A stumble. Then a thump as the body landed on the couch where she had just been.

"I know you're there, *hermanita*."

Relief poured over her, cool water on a sunburn. Even though she hated Diego. Even though he sounded drunk, which could end with shouts and fists.

"Go away."

An unsteady laugh. "Go fucking where?"

Back to your friends. To red bandannas. "I don't care."

"Yeah, I guess you don't," he said flatly.

There was silence as they both sat in the dark, her tucked into the corner beside the couch, hands around her knees. She imagined him sprawled out the way Daddy used to look, head resting back, tired and angry. Drunk.

His voice was quiet, barely loud enough to hear. "I fucked up."

It was enough to make her peer around the arm of the sofa. He wasn't sprawled back. His head rested in his hands. It shouldn't matter to her that he looked sad. She hated him.

At least, she was supposed to hate him. Part of her did.

"I know I fucked everything up," he continued, low and hoarse. "I'm sorry, Sofia. So fucking sorry."

Emotions were like hot oil in a pan; even from far away they could spatter and burn. She ran her hands over her shins, trying to brush it away. Failing. "Doesn't matter."

Another laugh. "Nice try. You know how much Dad would kick my ass if he was alive?"

"When he was drunk." When he was drunk he'd hit anyone.

Quiet. "Yeah. When he was drunk. I'd deserve it this time, though. Deserve a lot worse than that."

She didn't really disagree. In moments of anger, she thought about maybe punching him. Kicking him. The way she couldn't do when it was happening. Just as fast the anger would change, and she'd be huddled on the bathroom floor, eyes leaking, heaving into the toilet.

She set the bowl down on the carpet and crept out from the corner.

He didn't move while she sat beside him, leaving a foot of space.

"Should have protected you," he mumbled. "Those fuckers…those *hermanos*…they're not my family."

She didn't have anything to say back. Or maybe she had too much to say. Hate, love. He was her brother. It was his gang who had violated her, with their cruel smiles and red bandannas.

Yes, she hated him. Even if he was sorry now.

But if she had to sit on the couch, awake in the middle of the night, it was better not to do it alone.

Chapter Five

NSTEAD OF PULLING into the extra carport like he used to, Nate parked down the street. A habit from his job. Stay out of sight. Blend in with the surroundings. Keep an eye out for anything suspicious.

Like that white unmarked van beside the curb.

It meant nothing. This was a pretty safe-pocket neighborhood despite its proximity to downtown. No reason to think anything was wrong.

I just wanted to hear your voice.

What if she was in trouble? No, it was just a stupid phone call. He told himself that even as he sped up, weaving through the wooded lawns so he'd be less visible on his approach.

Man, he was going to feel like a chump if he showed up at her place only to find her in bed with some guy. He'd found so many of his clients' wives that way, he almost expected it. But if there was even a chance she needed his help, if she were hurt… He couldn't even consider that.

His head pounded; his throat went dry. Skill only got a soldier so far. Beyond that, he'd learned to trust his instincts, and they were going haywire. A sunny day in a pleasant neighborhood, and everything was still, as if even the squirrels and the birds were in hiding, the whole street holding its breath.

He paused behind a large oak, scanning the entrance and windows. A shadow moved behind the blinds in the bedroom. His mind could easily picture her gorgeous body, skin always bronze, dripping wet after a shower.

Or had that shadow been someone else?

Her patio and the one beneath it were identical, but unlike the bottom one, the vertical blinds to her patio were open, as usual. He'd always given her a hard time about that, how she'd give the neighbors a show if she padded to the kitchen for a drink of water in the middle of the night. There were no neighbors now, only him. And the person walking across her living room wasn't wearing an oversize longhorn T-shirt.

He was dressed in all black, with a matching ski mask.

Nate knew what fear felt like. He'd belly

crawled through the bug-infested jungle, watching bullets plunge into the mud beside his head. He'd been tied up and beaten in a shit-brick hut. As they brought a bat down on his knee, he'd thought *I'm going to die here* and he had come to terms with that. It was what a soldier did; he felt fear and pushed through it.

None of those experiences prepared him for the sight of an armed intruder in Sofia's apartment. His brain went fuzzy red with rage for a split second, his whole being consumed with the need to attack. Right the fuck now.

He didn't care for himself. They could fill him full of lead, and through the pure force of his fury, he'd live long enough to strangle them personally. But Sofia would be up there. She could get taken hostage or caught in the cross fire. He couldn't risk it.

If they were at all smart, they were keeping a watch on the main entrance to the building and on Sofia's door. Maybe it was dead bolted, and he couldn't shoot through that without risking shooting her. Neither could he pick the lock without getting himself shot through the door.

The best entrance was a surprise attack through the patio. Beside the stacked patios, yellow hydrangeas trailed up the sides. He'd climb the trellis that started from the bottom and hope it held his weight.

At the base of the trellis he paused, hearing a faint sound from inside. He cocked his head. A muted scream of pain followed. Female. *Sofia.* And it was coming from the first floor. There was no time to analyze why the hell she was downstairs instead of up. Judging from the distance of the scream, she was farther inside the lower apartment, not near the patio door. He shot through the patio door, aiming toward the ground, and then kicked in the rest of the glass.

Pushing through the blinds, he took in the scene. Sofia was on the ground, holding the side of her face. Another man lay beside her, wounded or dead. A man dressed in black stood over her, armed.

A single tap to the head and the armed man went down.

Sofia shrieked, but his attention was diverted when another asshole thundered down the stairs. Retrieving the knife from his boot, Nate ducked behind the divider wall and waited.

The man rushed into the kitchen, and Nate grabbed him by the neck, sticking him in the back. The liver, he judged based on the height. A fatal blow. The man choked on his own vomit, and Nate let him slide to the floor, turning him over and straddling his neck.

"Who sent you?" he demanded.

The man's eyes were already rolling back in his head. Damn. He hadn't meant to kill this one, at least not so soon. Not when he still needed information. He shook the man, and the bastard's eyes slowly focused on him.

"That's right. Who sent you?"

"Fuck you," he spat.

"Come on, I'm trying to help you here. We can do this easy or hard. Easy means I end this quickly. Hard means I let you bleed out. That pain you're feeling now? It only gets worse. Now tell me who sent you."

"I don't know anything, I swear. They don't tell us anything." Far too late, panic entered his eyes, but Nate hadn't been lying about the pain.

He'd seen enough men die this way—too many men.

Nate cocked his head. The soft sound of booted footfalls came from upstairs. A third intruder.

He looked at the man beneath him with pity. "Wrong answer."

A smooth cut sliced open his throat and put him out of his misery. Despite Nate's threat to make him suffer, he'd never been comfortable with animal abuse.

During the scuffle, Sofia had crawled into the corner. Now she huddled against the refrigerator, her cheek already swelling. *Goddamn it.* That son of a bitch had hit her. Now he wanted to kill the fucker all over again. The fear in her eyes wrenched his gut, but he couldn't focus on that now.

He handed her his Sig. "Anyone comes in here that isn't me, shoot 'em."

She stared at the weapon, nostrils flared. Finally, she took it with a tight nod. Good girl.

Not sparing another second, he cleared each room in the downstairs apartment and then made his way upstairs. He only had his knife now, but on a good day, he was more lethal this way. And this would be a good day. Blood pumped fast and hot through his veins, imbuing him with speed and strength. Rage tightened his vision. They came after his girl? The last thing they'd see was his face, bidding them good night. Simple as motherfucking pie.

The third man was searching her closet. He didn't even detect Nate's approach until the knife was resting against his jugular. Nate used his free hand to lock the man's elbow behind his back.

"Your friends are dead," Nate murmured against the man's ear.

The acidic stench of urine suffused the air as the man wet himself.

Nate chuckled softly. "Tell me what you know, and I might let you live."

"I can't... I don't... Please, I don't..."

The man babbled incoherently. Nate let the knife cut into his skin, just a nick.

"Now, now," Nate said. "This is important. I need you to focus. You can do that for me, right?"

"I don't know anything. They just paid us to bring them the laptop."

"And?" Nate twisted the man's elbow.

"And the girl," he gasped out. "Leave her body. Take a picture."

A picture for proof of death. His girl, dead. Rage blackened his vision. Nate forced himself to calm. "Tell me about the man who paid you. Who is he?"

"I swear I don't know. I don't know. I don't know."

Disgusted, Nate shook his head. Dark impulses tugged at him. He could make this man talk. Nothing was more persuasive than pain, and Nate knew how to apply it. But Sofia was waiting for him downstairs. Lovely, pure Sofia who shouldn't be anywhere near this.

With a clinical blow to the man's temple, he knocked him out. Dragging the bulky man downstairs, he felt the first twinges in his knee. The pain couldn't touch him now, flying high on adrenaline, but if he pushed too hard, the joint was liable to give out. He forced himself to slow down as he returned to the kitchen and tossed his charge into a kitchen chair.

Sofia was waiting where he'd left her, her back against a corner, clutching the gun. He hated that she saw him as a killer now, the way he saw himself, but he couldn't focus on that now. The bruise on her cheek had swelled, making his blood burn hot. Her bright, fear-stained eyes watched the man's head loll back in the chair.

Nate crouched over the man who'd been on the floor since the beginning, blood staining his shirt. He vaguely recognized him as her landlord—what was his name, Ernie? He was always sniffing around Sofia's skirts. He touched his fingers to Ernie's pulse: dead and cooling. Well, he wouldn't need his belt then.

Nate removed it quickly and twined it through the back of the chair, binding his unconscious captive's hands behind his back. He stuck the top of the chair underneath the lip of the counter for good measure. The intruder probably wouldn't wake up for hours, but if he did, he'd be trapped.

When he turned back, Sofia held out a circle of duct tape. For reasons unknown, speech was beyond him at the moment. He raised an eyebrow.

"For…" She bit her lip. "For a blindfold. If you wanted."

Jesus. Her eyes were wide as saucers as he took it from her and tied it around the man's head. This had to be freaking her out, but she kept up just fine. But that was Sofia, capable and so damn gorgeous she made his heart squeeze painfully. He had the trained ability to shut off his emotions and become this violent machine. She didn't have that—just an innate sense of right and wrong and a courage that continually stunned him. Even after what she had been through, she wanted to fight for other people.

He bound the man's ankles to the legs of the chair for good measure. The homemade binds would keep the man contained until police arrived. He stepped back and surveyed the man. Black T-shirt, black cargo pants. No identification. He may not have been the highest quality, but there was no doubt he'd spoken the truth—he was a paid mercenary.

In Sofia's closet, a paid mercenary.

Using the kitchen phone, he placed a call directly to his buddy on the Austin police force. The man had been Special Forces before Nate's time, but the respect was mutual. They'd had an off-the-records understanding, with Jed providing information when Nate needed it and Nate following up on leads when Jed's hands were tied up with red tape.

"This is Lieutenant Commander Patterson." The answer was clipped.

"Jed. It's Nate."

"Nate." His voice sharpened, detecting the thinly veiled violence in Nate's voice. "What's wrong?"

"I need some uniforms over here." He rattled off the address. "A few men down. Another one's my gift to you. They broke into Sofia's place. Assaulted her. Killed her landlord."

"Shit." There was rustling. "I'll put in the call, but it may be a while."

Seriously? "I've got a prisoner in fucking leather bondage and duct tape. Not to mention a few cooling bodies. Let's make this sooner rather than later."

"I hear you, but we're drowning. Code fucking red. Haven't you heard?"

"Tell me."

Nate's blood ran cold as he listened. An explosion at the *Austin Daily*, where Sofia worked. He stared into her fathomless dark brown eyes across the few feet of kitchen tile that separated them while Jed told him all about the blast that could have killed her. That darkening bruise on her cheek was nothing compared to what a bomb could do to her. He had no idea what had happened to make her a target, but he was going to keep her safe.

He didn't take his eyes off hers when he spoke. "Jed? I'm leaving the prisoner for you, but when your guys get here, we'll be gone."

"You need to remain there. Someone will need to take your statement—"

"This is my statement, Jed. These fuckers were in her apartment. Her motherfucking *closet*. And now you tell me they bombed her work? I'm not letting her stick around to give them a third shot at her."

The line was quiet a moment; then Jed said, "Yeah. Okay."

And *yeah, okay* because Jed knew who Sofia was to him. Which meant he also knew that Nate wasn't going to let a damn thing happen to her.

An explosion at her work and three mercenaries in her home? Jesus.

He hung up the phone.

On impulse, he strode over and pulled her into his arms. He was dirty and she was clean, but he couldn't resist holding her tight, breathing in her hair and feeling her pulse beat beneath soft skin. Her breath came in rapid puffs against his shirtfront. Alive. She was alive. And yeah, he was trembling; he could own that, because if he hadn't been here, if he'd never seen her again, he'd have lost it.

So much for pretending he didn't give a damn. Every cell in his body was attuned to her— her safety, her fear. His concern for her was all-encompassing, leaving him…exactly where he'd always avoided. Open. Vulnerable.

She turned her face up, her gaze searching his. He had no idea what she saw there, but it made her cup her palm against his jaw. It was clenched tight, but at her touch, he loosened a fraction, at the proof that she wasn't afraid of him after what she'd seen him do.

"Is this why you wouldn't tell me?" she whispered.

Towards the end, she'd tried to get him to tell her about his time in the army. Things that he was careful to avoid speaking about, even thinking about, things that only surfaced occasionally in his dreams.

He had refused, of course. The reason why they sent trained killers out into the world was so people like her could be safe and ignorant in their beds. She might have thought she wanted to know, but he wouldn't wish that knowledge on anyone.

It was the same reason he'd never told her about his moonlighting gig—the black ops work he still did on the side. Even though the omission had meant he'd never be truly open with her, had maybe caused the rift between them that made her walk.

Yes, this was a glimpse of what it had been like, skimming the surface of death and darkness and the despair that he really was a coldhearted bastard.

He turned her question around. "Why didn't you tell me about the explosion?"

She flinched. The irony didn't escape him that he expected her to confide in him while he kept his past locked up. But that was ancient history and this was her life at stake. Nothing was more important than that.

"It doesn't feel real." Her brow lowered in

confusion. "I was right outside. I watched it happen, but it doesn't seem real."

He understood that. The first time he'd watched three of his buddies blown to bits in an IED explosion, he'd kept expecting to see them in their bunks. When they'd assigned other soldiers to their beds, Nate had started a cafeteria brawl with one of them, as if he could punch the truth of the matter right out of him. Didn't work though.

It sucked to care. Sucked a lot, and Sofia cared more than anyone he knew.

He couldn't find the words to tell her it got easier, couldn't lie to her when she seemed so small and fragile in his arms. After the fight, his commanding officer had looked at him with knowing eyes, when Nate hadn't even understood why he was so pissed off.

As punishment, he'd been assigned to scrub the decks for a week, but the labor had been exactly what he'd needed to get his head on straight. Something to keep busy and be useful.

That was all he could offer Sofia.

"Go pack a bag," he said.

She blinked slowly. "Why?"

"We're getting out of here, at least for tonight. Until I can figure out what the hell's going on and how to keep you safe."

He braced himself for her objections. She would want to talk to the police, give a statement. Have them protect her instead of her bastard ex-boyfriend. But the argument never came. She simply went upstairs to do as he asked. He followed her, humbled by her blind trust in him and unwilling to let her out of his sight.

She packed quickly, bringing only a backpack with clothes and toiletries and a messenger bag.

"Your laptop in there?" he asked, nodding toward the bag.

She glanced down. "Yeah, why?"

Because she'd almost been killed for it. "Do you always bring it with you to work?"

"Sometimes. I've got a desktop there, but I wanted to bring some files home. The images can get pretty huge, so it's fastest to download them directly to my laptop."

"Well, that's what the men were after." That and a snapshot of a hole in her head, but he didn't think that part needed elaboration at the moment.

She frowned, lifting the flap to peek at her laptop. "I don't know what would be valuable. A bunch of newspaper clippings that are publicly available."

"Hmm. We'll look through it when you're

safe."

He kept her behind him down the stairs and across the lawns to his car. Most likely those men were it. Three would have seemed like plenty to kill an unarmed young woman. But he wasn't taking any chances.

He gestured her into the driver's seat.

She raised her eyebrows in surprise but threw her bags into the passenger seat and sat behind the wheel without complaint. It warmed him that she seemed to trust him still, even after seeing what he was capable of. Then again, she'd never balked at following his orders—at least in one area of their relationship.

He handed her the keys and watched while she turned on the ignition. "I'm going to scope out the van I think they came in. Most likely no one's in there or they would have bolted when the shooting started, but just in case, I want you to stay here with the engine running. If anyone approaches the car that's not me—"

"Run them over?"

He felt a grin tug at his lips. "I was going to say hightail it out of here, but that works too."

Chapter Six

SOFIA TRIED NOT to stare at him. He hadn't told her what he'd seen in the van, but it wasn't good. He'd radiated tension when he got back to the car and ordered her into the passenger seat. Now his attention was on the road as they crossed a single-lane suspension bridge.

The rich hues of ink spilled from beneath his sleeves, the worn fabric of his shirt clinging to packed muscle. The light brown hair on his face had grown longer than she was used to, and she knew that it would leave marks on her private places if they had still been together.

He didn't turn as he spoke. "Give me your phone."

Part of her wanted to refuse him, but clearly he knew what he was doing and she was out of her depth. Besides, he was pretty attractive when he got all commanding. Comforting too. After the terror of the explosion and then the intruders in her house, it felt damn good to have him there.

When she handed over her iPhone, he popped out the SIM card, rolled down the window of his Trans Am, and tossed it over the side of the bridge. So they couldn't be tracked. She wasn't trained the way he was, but she'd paid enough attention as a reporter and watched enough action flicks to follow what he was doing.

He handed back the phone, and she slipped it into her bag, though it was just a fancy hunk of silicone now. She wondered if she could still get at her contact list. That was the only thing of importance here anyway. Everything else was on the *Daily*'s servers—or on her laptop. The laptop she'd almost died for.

She shuddered, forcing her thoughts away. The events at the *Daily* and at her apartment were still unreal, and she preferred them that way. Reality was horrifying. This quiet bubble with Nate—this was where she wanted to stay.

All of her was cold, the chill settled deep in her bones and icing all around her, so that she watched the world through a cracked-crystal lens. The distance was a good thing. A safe thing. Like watching the blades of a lazy ceiling fan turn, tucked beneath heavy blankets.

She couldn't afford to break down right now.

That would be for later, when Nate wasn't so

close, so…intense.

He had barely spared her a glance, but she got the impression that he was finely attuned to his surroundings, including her. He was handling this situation with a capability she'd never doubted but hadn't seen firsthand. It was her problem, and he was fixing it. She wouldn't make this harder by sobbing in his car.

His hair was longer now, the ends glowing orange in the waning daylight. She wanted to touch it, to run her fingers through it. To see if he'd let her lead his body with a fistful of it the way he'd once done with her hair. Probably not, though. He didn't submit, and damn if she didn't like him that way. Not to mention the fact that his stubbornness had probably saved her life today.

"How'd you know to come see me?" she asked softly.

He slanted her a wry glance. "You know why I came."

And maybe she did know. She'd dithered on the phone, too afraid to ask for comfort from the man she'd kicked to the curb. But he had understood the implicit invitation, the barely banked need for reassurance after seeing the explosion. Of course, instead of a hot shower and hotter sex, he'd shown up at her door, guns blazing.

Her hero, even though he hated that word.

The trees grew denser, the lanes more narrow as the old car wound higher into north Austin. Not toward downtown, where first response teams would be dealing with the aftermath. Not toward his small office in a historic south Austin house and his apartment upstairs.

"Where are we going?" she finally asked.

"A friend's house."

She pondered that a minute. His tone didn't exactly invite conversation, but although she was willing to be a passenger in this, she needed to understand what was happening. It was part of her innate curiosity, something Nate enjoyed in certain, more carnal pursuits, but which had ultimately been their downfall. She was always asking questions, always grasping, always reaching up the goddamn ladder, when he had chained himself to the bottom rung in some sort of protest against the world.

"I thought we'd go to your place."

He shook his head. "The phone call. You called me after the blast. Even if they didn't know about our…past relationship, they could pull the phone records and find out about me."

"And your house," she finished quietly. "Oh, Nate. I'm so sorry. I really didn't think—"

He snorted. "You are *not* going to apologize for getting attacked by hit men. Of course you didn't plan for that. No one would have."

Well, maybe not most people, but he seemed pretty well prepared for all contingencies. That was different, though. *He* was different. She was sure it had never even occurred to him not to help. Risk his life to protect her. Drop everything he had going on to keep her safe. Anything she needed, of course, of course. No wonder she'd fallen for him so hard.

It was only real life that had gotten in the way.

The old engine struggled up the steep hills until finally he turned off onto a small, dark road. A little way down, the headlights illuminated a one-story house, but she wasn't fooled by its height. This was a luxury neighborhood, where even a shack would sell for half a mil.

He cut the engine.

"Your friend lives here?"

His laugh was soft but rich in the darkness. "Don't think I know any rich people? I know plenty of them. They pay me to spy on their wives."

"You did not bring me to a client's house."

She hoped not.

He got out, pulling her bags out from his side. "Nah, an old army buddy. Who's done real well, obviously. I'm just keeping an eye on the house until tomorrow."

She followed him to the two wide front doors, metal with rivets spread across them for industrial decoration. He unlocked the door, then disabled an alarm system interface that looked more advanced than her laptop.

Inside, the living area was a huge open plan. Sleek modern furniture was slung across a smooth, dark wood floor. The house was thin, probably conforming to the steep, rocky land it sat on. The back wall was almost entirely glass, showing off the view—miles of hilly treetops sprinkled with the occasional light from another expensive home.

"Wow," she breathed. *Really well* had been an understatement.

"Right?" He fiddled with the thermostat, and the AC kicked in with a soft whoosh. "That's what a little private security work can get you."

Private security, sure, but she bet this guy had contracts with the government. Black ops.

"You could probably work for your friend," she said. Heck, he'd been given the keys to the guy's house—literally. That showed trust.

He gave a short laugh. "I don't need that kind of headache."

Of course, because he didn't want to protect her. Didn't want to protect anyone. What he really meant was that *she* was the headache. And he didn't need her. He'd proven that much when he'd let her walk away.

Chapter Seven

A FLAT-SCREEN TV stretched over the southern wall.

Stung from Nate's words, she wandered across thick planks of glossy dark wood and found the remote. *I don't need that kind of headache.*

"At least thirty people have been reported injured as a result of the blast that shook the *Daily* newspaper offices this morning, two in critical condition. There are no reported fatalities at this time."

Sofia watched the solemn expression and emphatic gestures of the newscaster. Laura Meade. She'd met her once at a media awards dinner a year ago. Her impression had been large hair and deep red lipstick, though they looked almost ordinary on the TV screen.

She'd known early on that TV wasn't right for her. Her shaky hands now seemed to confirm it. She could write about dark things from the safety of her desk, but she couldn't be in the action with perfect nails and a tight smile.

Except now the sanctity of the office had been violated.

Warm hands closed around her shoulders, and she jumped. Nate squeezed gently, then ran his hands down her arms. She was shocked to feel the heat of him, shocked to realize how cold she'd gotten.

He sat down and pulled her into his lap without a word. *Are you okay? Everything will be fine.* He didn't give her false platitudes. He'd been in a freaking war zone. He knew she wasn't okay.

He knew everything might not be fine.

Who was in critical condition? "I want to call Remy."

Even without seeing him, she knew the slight motion. *No.*

But she needed to know what was happening. "I won't tell her where I am."

"They came after you," he said roughly. "I could have lost you today. Don't tell me I have to risk you again. Not now. I won't fucking do it."

And she realized she wasn't the only one who wasn't okay.

She turned in his arms, looking up at him. Her forehead touched his, their breaths mingled. He gripped her sides so tightly she thought there'd be bruises, and that was fine. Bruises meant pain. Pain meant life. *I could have lost you today.*

She could have lost him too.

"Nate," she murmured.

He made a wordless sound, a denial. "I know you don't want this, but I have to—"

His words cut off abruptly, as if he couldn't help himself. Warm lips. Searing tongue. His kiss came quick and forced, pushing her mouth open, claiming what she'd taken away.

Just as suddenly, he shoved her back, pushing her onto the sofa.

She panted, staring into the dark turmoil of his eyes.

The TV filled the space between them. "The Austin Police Department have issued a statement confirming the pinpoint of the blast as the data center of the newspaper. No terrorist organizations have taken responsibility for the attacks."

"No one's going to," she whispered quietly.

Nate's expression hardened. "You know who did it."

"Not for sure."

"Someone came after *your* laptop after destroying the *Daily*'s data center. They're after information that you have. They're after *you.*"

She shivered. "I'm working on a big story."

"Of course you are," he said flatly, running a hand through his unruly hair.

This had been the argument between them, how she had cared so much. How he had cared so little. At least, he pretended not to. She could have lived with that, but she couldn't have lived with him keeping her locked up like some fragile bird. She had already been locked up once. She wouldn't go back, for anyone. Not even him.

"And you won't stop." It wasn't a question.

She swallowed hard. "This is everything to me."

"Jesus, Sofia." Walls came down over his brown eyes, his expressive lips, the long scruff on his face. He was closing off to her again, and it was her fault. She couldn't pretend otherwise. They were at an impasse, again. They'd been here before.

If she didn't have this drive to find justice…

If he didn't care so damn much about her getting hurt…

"Thank you," she whispered.

His eyes narrowed. "Don't fucking start."

"Why not? You saved my life." Tears filled her eyes.

He made a low growling sound. "Fuck no.

We're not doing this. I'm not some godforsaken hero. And you're sure as hell not helpless."

She struggled to hold back the tears, her lower lip trembling. "I know that. But those men. It was too much like—I thought—"

He stood up and swung away from her, his muscles rigid, vibrating. "If your brother weren't dead, I'd fucking kill him again. He wasn't a fucking hero. And neither am I."

Her brother had died protecting her.

She didn't want Nate to die.

This was how they'd broken up before, Sofia wanting Nate to care, to believe in something. Nate wanting her to quit the paper, quit fighting. Quit caring like him.

She stood up stiffly, feeling broken all over again. The scrapes from falling on concrete, the bruises he'd left on her hips. Nothing hurt as deeply as seeing the regret on his face that he'd kissed her, held her.

"You don't have to watch out for me," she said.

"Yes, I do," he said grimly, and it sounded more like a threat than a kindness.

Guilt churned her stomach. "I'm really sorry."

"We're not back to that, are we?" He stood up and turned away from her. "Someone can damn well apologize for using up three of my bullets, but that someone isn't you. Now come over here. Let's take a look at your laptop and see what's so valuable."

Swallowing past her hurt, she turned off the TV and followed him to the kitchen—an open space without break from the living room. He spun a simple oak chair around and straddled it, casual. Maybe even professional. Nothing like that urgent kiss. That wouldn't happen again.

She had to remember that this was only temporary. Very temporary if his friend was coming back tomorrow. They'd figure out a game plan, and then she'd be on her own again.

Alone again.

She pulled out her laptop and set it up on the thick oak table. He watched while she booted up and typed in her password. The desktop appeared, with the background picture of a long, winding stream wedged between two vertical rock faces. It was a pretty panorama of the Shoal Creek park, no people in the picture, but suddenly she remembered exactly what they'd done on the day they'd taken the picture, and from the heated look on his face, he did too.

It was a public park but lush with trees and rock formations. Not very populated either. They had splashed in a shallow bend, him in shorts only and her in a bikini, slipping over the rocky bottom until he'd decided to see whether the current could be used to good advantage. He'd spread her folds with slick fingers, letting the water rush across her clit. She'd come hard, her shouts echoing off the rock faces.

That had been fun and games, though. Not like now.

Now she watched the scruffy line of his neck as he swallowed. Her gaze slipped down his arms, his waist, admiring the angles that made up his body. When naked, he was all straight shadows and swooping lines, as if he were charcoal-drawn right in front of her and filled in with breath. He didn't think he was a hero, didn't even like the word, but God, his patriotism, his passion was written on every inch of his skin. The stars and stripes on the side of his torso, the eagle on his biceps. The Army Ranger shield on his back with intricate scrollwork, the names of his fallen team members scripted amid the scars on his body. He should have seemed bulky, his large frame on the almost dainty chair, but he moved with grace, even when his knee was bothering him.

It was bothering him now. His thumb was absently running over the fabric of his jeans. The events of this afternoon must have aggravated his injury. She wanted to ask him to elevate his leg, to take off those constricting jeans and have her massage away the swelling, but he wouldn't agree to any of that. He liked to pretend that nothing could hurt him, that nothing could touch him. No man was an island, but he'd built a pretty impressive moat.

She met his eyes and found he'd been watching her. He'd seen her check him out and the desire in her eyes.

His voice had gone hoarse when he said, "Show me where you keep your work files."

"It's all in here. It's organized by the topic here and then split into research, photos, and the actual articles within." She flipped through a few of her more recent articles to illustrate, then turned the laptop sideways so he could take over.

"How do you back this up?"

"I don't, really." She stood and rummaged through the freezer, pulling out a bag of frozen peas. "I know that's not good, but I use the *Daily* as my backup. If my laptop crashed, all the important stuff would still be on their servers."

"But if the servers at the *Daily* were to become…unavailable, this would be the only copy left?"

She frowned, tearing off a few paper towels. "Well, maybe. But only certain files. Other reporters would keep their stuff on their computers."

"So this has to do with one of your stories. And in your gut, you already know which one. Tell me."

Damn. She did have a few open projects, as usual. The exposé on the city park permit forgery was getting dicey. But her gut had lasered in on the Moreland case pretty much as soon as she'd seen the smoke rising. That was the only story big enough to warrant this magnitude of violence, though it still shocked her.

She'd stepped on a land mine, and her friends had suffered the blast. While intellectually she understood that she wasn't responsible for the actions of criminals, regret tasted bitter in her mouth.

"Senator Moreland. I think he's dirty."

"Dirty how?"

"Drugs. Human trafficking. Really bad stuff."

He whistled. "The guy who's running for president? That Moreland?"

She returned to her seat, pressing the paper-towel-wrapped bag of frozen peas against his knee. He looked up in surprise, the look in his eyes unfathomable.

They were inches apart; she lowered her voice. "That one."

He gently took the bag from her. "How long have you been investigating into him?"

She opened her mouth to answer just as he pressed the makeshift ice pack to her face. She winced at the soft pressure, the soft rebuff of her care. He wouldn't let her take care of him now. She'd lost that right when she'd lost him.

"Only a couple of months," she answered, her voice coming out husky. "I thought I'd been careful, framing every interview from the campaign finance angle so no one knew I suspected more. Not careful enough, though."

He turned back to the laptop, leaving the bag in her hands. Fingers flying over the keyboard, he quickly found the right folder and began reading the contents of her latest research notes.

Page down, page down, fast even if he was only scanning, and she knew he was soaking up the information. She'd seen him do it before with his own private investigator work, glance at a report and pick out the pertinent information when she would need to pore over it, to sort and weigh all the parts in her mind before coming to the same conclusions.

Even though she knew it to be false, she still occasionally fell prey to the don't-give-a-fuck exterior he portrayed. It was in moments like this, when he was too engrossed in his work, that he forgot to cover his tracks. Moments like in her apartment, fighting with the ferocity of an avenging angel, that she could see him as he really was.

He closed her research notes and clicked over to the photos. The most recent ones were the articles the intern had scanned for her. They flashed on the screen, unreadable at the smaller size, some diagonal and a few upside down. If there was anything special, it would take some time to figure it out. More than a night. The newspaper clippings gave way to documents.

"Those are all public records," she said. "Anyone could have ordered them."

"But no one else did, I'm betting. Only you."

And look what it had done. She turned her face away as he clicked through the rest of them. How many people had been harmed in that blast? And Ernie. She would have to live with that.

"Why are these files so big?"

She glanced back, where he was looking at the file list of photos. "I have no idea. A lot of times the images we use for the paper are big. I wouldn't even pay attention, but they take a long time to download."

"Yeah, if there are photographs going into print, they're probably high resolution. But these are just scanned newspaper images. Grainy too. Though even if they were high resolution, it wouldn't explain these numbers. A whole application would be this size. Or a lot of data."

She sometimes forgot, too, that he'd had pretty advanced training as a member of the army's Special Forces. The physical training was at the forefront of her mind—how could it not be with that hard body? And more recently, his precision handling with weapons, his gun, his knife. The duct tape wasn't exactly professional combat equipment, as far as she knew, but he'd seemed pretty comfortable restraining a prisoner as well.

He also knew his way around technology. More than her, that was for certain.

"Is there a way to see what the data is?" she asked.

He opened a console window and typed. Text and symbols flashed on the screen. "Nah. It's all just bytecode, not readable text. I know a guy who might be able to figure out what's in here though. I can send these files over to him. The network here is secure, and we can trust him."

It seemed to be a question, so she nodded.

He knew a lot of guys. The house, the tech stuff. He was a walking problem-solving shop, and he wanted to pretend he was just some shoot-the-shit slacker? She could have laughed, it was so ludicrous.

Instead she kissed his cheek. The bristle was long enough to tickle her lips instead of abrade them.

His breath caught. "It's getting late. You can hit the sack while I send this off."

She swallowed her disappointment. He still wanted her; she knew that. But he was pushing her away. "Think it'll be okay if I grab a shower?"

"Sure." He nodded to the right. "The bedroom's that way."

"Okay." She was curious about the sleeping arrangements, whether there were multiple guest rooms or if they'd use the same one. But it seemed likely she'd get rebuffed at the moment, with him typing furiously and already focused on the task at hand.

Grabbing her backpack from the floor by the entrance, she headed down the hall. And was shocked to find there was only one bedroom here. A very large master bedroom with an almost equally large bathroom. Prompted by her damned curiosity, she poked her head into the main area.

"Is there another bedroom on the other side of the house?"

He didn't look up from his work. "It's set up as an office."

"So, wait a minute. This house, which probably cost more money than I'll ever make, has only one bedroom."

He grinned as he glanced up. "Hey, don't look at me that way. I didn't buy it."

I don't need that kind of headache.

No, he wasn't interested in black ops or high-paying secret jobs. He wasn't interested in her. She had to remember that. And maybe it was for the best, because a job like that would be dangerous. Those moments in her apartment proved that much.

CHAPTER EIGHT

THE SHOWER WAS big enough to fit five people, with two showerheads and a line of smaller nozzles down each side. It was distracting actually; she was used to the small, rather forceful spray that came out of her little nozzle at home. Eventually, the warm water worked its magic, loosening her muscles and turning the blood pumping through her veins to sludge.

She wished Nate would join her. He wouldn't.

Not in the shower, not in bed. Despite the one-bedroom situation, she was sure he'd attempt to wedge his long body onto the small square-edged leather couch in the main area. He may have shown up ready to defend her, but he didn't want her again.

Leave it alone, Sofia.

Except the curiosity had caught hold of her. That little hitch in his breath when she'd kissed his cheek. She remembered that same sound from before—when she kissed his mouth, when she kissed his chest, when she kissed the tip of his cock. It meant he was hard and ready and wanting, so why did he push her away?

For the same reasons they'd separated, most likely.

The damned real world again, intruding.

This wasn't the real world, this luxurious friend's house with its granite sinks and oak rafters. She didn't even feel real, just wispy and half-formed, like she could rinse away down the drain if she didn't hold it together.

She recognized the signs of shock in herself.

Her chest felt tight, her muscles aching, everywhere. She needed sleep, but she was way too wired. If she lay down, she'd only replay the horrible scenes she'd been trying to block out. The spray of dust when she'd turned her face toward the explosion. The crack of the intruder's fist against her face. The splatter of blood against the cabinets as he'd fallen.

No. She wanted to feel alive, proof that this wasn't some sort of waking dream, walking around after she was dead without even knowing it. She wanted to feel her breath, her body, instead of just floating above them.

She wanted Nate.

Stepping out of the shower, she gave herself a cursory pat down, knowing he appreciated the shine of her wet skin. He liked to lick each droplet of water from her, working his way down and then teasing her that she kept getting *more* wet, not less.

He was sitting where she'd left him, at the kitchen table in the large open space. He rubbed his palm over his jaw in that way of his, the one that said he was stressed and tired and needed release she was ready to provide. They both needed this.

She crossed the wood floor. It was chilly beneath her feet, the cold shooting up her legs, pebbling her skin, and making her nipples hard before she'd even reached him. He turned as she approached.

His whole body tensed, eyes dark and threatening. "What are you doing?"

She would live if he rejected her. At least that was what she told herself.

Instead he felt like some vital part of her she needed back. A deep breath after being underwater for so long, strands of sunlight through the surface her only source of warmth.

"We were always good at this part," she whispered.

Lines formed between his eyes. He kept his gaze glued to hers, eyes dark with intensity. "It's not a good idea, Sofia."

"Why not?"

"If I touch you, I may not be able to stop."

He was so careful with her. Once, *careful* had been the only way she could let a man touch her. He'd been the one to teach her pleasure. The one to teach her trust. The one to show her that rough could feel good too. "Then don't stop."

"You don't know what you're asking for. These months without having you, without—" His voice broke on a rough sound.

Without what? Her mind flinched away from the thought of him with someone else, but he might have moved on. He might have only come to protect her, his heart taken by someone else. Someone with more courage than her.

"Did you…move on?" she asked softly.

His eyes darkened. "Move on? I haven't touched anyone else, Sofia. I can't touch anyone else. I can't even *look* at anyone else. I'm yours, whether I'm with you or not."

Then she couldn't wait anymore. She ran her fingers through his hair, finally touching the satiny strands. Using her grip on his hair, she tilted his head up. Maybe she'd been wrong about his ability to submit in bed, because he followed her tacit order and looked his fill. His tongue slipped out along his lips, and she knew he was imagining tasting her, sucking her. Hell, *she* was imagining it. Already slick and ready for it.

His voice had dropped. "I can't take advantage of you. You're tired and scared and—"

"I'm not scared of you." He wasn't anything like those men, those red bandannas.

She stepped into the circle of his arms, his breath, and felt warmer than a hundred hot showers; she felt whole. He thought he wasn't a hero? God, he couldn't stop protecting her—even from himself.

She wanted so badly to lose herself in him, to be as she was in bed with him—nothing but a woman being loved by a man. No complicated life drama, no dangerous men out to kill her. Just a stream of groans and shudders and kisses all along the rough-haired skin of his body.

"I want what we had before," she whispered.

His eyes closed on a groan that sounded like pain. "Sofia…"

A flicker of concern pierced her haze. "Is it your knee? Is it hurting bad?"

His laugh was raw. When his eyes opened, there was a feral gleam. "You think a busted knee is going to keep me from you? I could break every bone in my body and still fuck you just fine. I could be broken to shit, but I could still make you come with just my tongue."

Her body turned liquid at the memory of his tongue against her folds. "Then why?"

"It's my heart that won't survive you, gorgeous."

She barely had time to process the words before he was moving, a blur of masculine skin and muscle. In a flash he was standing over her, around her, and his knee seemed to be working very well as he backed her against a wall and shoved his leg between hers.

"Do you need to come, Sofia? Is that the problem? You only had to ask. I'll always take care of you." His hands roamed her slick skin, one cupping the back of her neck, the other sliding in a sinuous curve down her breasts, her hips, and curling back up to where his leg spread her open.

The first touch of his finger was like the gong of a bell, reverberating through her body. She'd expected their physical connection to center her, to bring her back into her body, but just the opposite was happening. She was floating away, becoming all sensation.

He added another finger, still lightly stroking

her sex, gently probing. Though her body clamored for more, faster, now, she clutched his arms and submitted to his languid pace. The longer he spent on her, the harder she would come. The more he touched her, the faster she could forget.

Finally he slipped one finger inside, then two, teasing the entrance.

"Tight," he said, nipping at her earlobe. "So fucking tight."

She moaned in response.

His breath puffed cool against the damp skin of her neck. "Haven't you been working yourself with that toy? I know how much you liked it."

Her breath caught. The purple one that reached right to her G-spot. He'd bought it for her when they'd first been together, when he had taught her about pleasure and all the ways she could find it. With his fingers, his mouth. With the thick toy as he leaned over her, thrusting it inside her until she came. He sucked her nipples the whole time, whispering how sexy she was, how wet. It had been weeks of orgasms, her body strung out, before he'd finally made love to her.

But the plastic was too hard, too impersonal after they split up.

Now his fingers slipped deeper, seeking the

same spot within her. And finding it. *Ohhhh,* her hips bucked into his hand. He stroked her there with the same maddeningly slow rhythm. Just one leisurely caress followed by another while she was frantic and urgent and whimpering into his mouth.

"Well, Sofia? Have you been using it?"

"No," she moaned. "Just the…the vibrator."

The little bullet-shaped vibrator pressed to her clit would get her off quickly. Her climax was never as hard as with the purple toy—or with Nate. Just a moment's relief before bedtime.

"I like that one too," he said, and his thumb found her clit. He didn't play there, just rested his thumb as his fingers worked inside her, and the dual pressure pulled her up on her toes, drew her whole body up tight.

"I want—I want—"

"What is it? If you don't ask for it, I can't give it to you. Do you need to come?"

She babbled. "Oh God, I do. I need to come. Please, please. Make me come."

"That's good, gorgeous." The appreciation in his voice was warm and rich. "That's my girl."

Then he dropped his head and sucked on her nipples. He knew exactly what she needed, playing her body, winding her tighter until she broke apart, spilling wetness onto his hand, clenching around his fingers, and grasping at his long, silky hair, as she distantly heard his muttered encouragement, *yeah, that's right, take it.*

He brought her down slowly, letting her cling to him, caressing her quivering muscles to soothe her. He was always this way, seeing to her needs first, usually multiple times, before he'd tell her he couldn't take it anymore and then guide her to her knees or spread her legs to take his pleasure. She reached for the buckle of his jeans, but he pushed her hand away.

She froze.

Had she misjudged the entire thing? If he truly wasn't interested in her and she had pushed him—but no. Her fingers had brushed against the hard ridge of his cock through the denim. His desire for her felt as strong as ever, only sharpened now, hurting her now.

Maybe, maybe…she started to slide down the wall. On her knees, she could please him, and oh, how eager she was to lose herself that way. She fumbled at his zipper until he caught her wrists. For a second, she wasn't sure what he would do with them. He seemed unsure, as well. Maybe hold them above her head and direct the whole thing himself—and yes, that was fine with her too.

But he released them and turned away, breathing hard. She reached out her hand, saw that it was shaking, and let it fall. This was how it had been when they were new, when she'd been scared of sex, when he'd been scared of hurting her. They'd moved past this, hadn't they?

Maybe they had to start over.

"Nathaniel?" she asked. Her voice was shaking too, the tremors running deep into her soul.

The silence was tense with unspent arousal and an anger she couldn't understand—didn't want to understand.

"Ask me again." His voice deepened into a growl.

"What?"

"Ask me again, any other night, any other day when you didn't almost die three times before dinner."

She rocked back on her heels, letting her head fall against the wall. *Oh no. Oh Nate.* She was using him and worse—worst of all, he knew it. He understood the blissful refuge she found in his body and the way she had demanded it to chase away the pain and fear of the day. And he'd let her. She couldn't think about that directly, didn't want to know what it meant that he would let himself be a warm, hard body to get her off while refusing any pleasure for himself.

The tears wouldn't be held back then. They poured over her cheeks, fast and copious because they'd been inside for so long. Her friends were gone. The *Daily* was gone. Her whole life—gone, gone, gone. There weren't any sobs; she was one tight mass of useless woman, just clenched and hopeless and grieving.

"Breathe, Sofia," he said, low and lilting. He pulled her into his arms, rubbing her back in slow circles. "Breathe."

She sucked in a sharp lungful of air, but that only made it worse. The space between them smelled like Nate and sex, and that was all wrong. This wasn't refuge, it was cowardice, taking her pleasure from a man who would give and give and give until he had nothing left, and then just walk away like he didn't care, as if he expected nothing better than that anyway.

That was what he had done for the army, and then they had turned him away. Rejected for the injuries he'd gotten during service. She had done the same thing, the same horrible thing, and the tears came even faster, her breath nothing but choked apologies. *I'm sorry I used you. I'm sorry I let you go. I'm sorry, sorry, sorry…*

"No, gorgeous," he murmured, holding her tighter. It was only when he really crushed her that she felt she could breathe again. "Don't be sorry. I'm here. I know. I know." And every soft *I know* replaced her hollow apologies, because he did know. He knew what it was like to see friends hurt, the horror and the helplessness and the traitorous relief that at least she was still safe, even though they weren't.

She felt his erection, thick and painful against her hip, but she understood. It was just a physical reaction, like her tears. She couldn't control her body; she couldn't control a world intent on hurting her. But she could choose this. She could choose *him,* and so she clung to his body as she cried, tethering herself to a mast while the storm ripped and clawed all around them.

He rocked her body and stroked her hair until her eyelids felt puffy and far too heavy to ever stay open. She drifted in that place, knowing no harm would come to her so long as he held her and wishing this moment could last forever. She was already asleep, she thought, when she heard him murmur, "I missed you so much."

Chapter Nine

REMY STARED INTO her Styrofoam cup. Was gray an appropriate color for coffee? She gulped it down, too exhausted to go searching for the vending machines again. All the hallways looked the same, and last time it had taken her twenty minutes to find her way back to the waiting room.

Not that it had mattered. Nothing changed. Not in twenty minutes, not in ten hours. The answer was the same. *We can't disclose that information.*

When the nurses' shifts changed, she'd convinced the new head nurse that she was Andre's girlfriend. It had felt like a lie, how she'd sometimes make up stories to get some information for an article. Really, she'd been lying most of her life. But this had been kind of the truth, wasn't it? She didn't do labels, but this was the closest thing she'd had to an actual relationship in a long, long time—maybe ever.

He would have taken her out on dates too. He'd asked, repeatedly. But she'd insisted on sticking to hurried sex in his office under the guise of getting in trouble. It had seemed like the right thing to do at the time. Men got to have office affairs without repercussions or expectations for more, so she wanted that too.

Plus, it was more convenient that way. She could get information from him in that post-orgasmic stupor. And since he never saw her outside work, he'd never question all the terse phone calls that came in at odd hours.

But now that she was faced with losing him, she wished everything had been different. That she'd agreed to go catch a movie with him instead of locking the door and crawling under his desk for an illicit blowjob—even if it had made both of them hot at the time. She wished she'd never snooped in his contact list for anonymous sources. That she'd never set the ball in motion that had resulted in the explosion at the *Daily*'s offices.

Her phone buzzed. She glanced at the large NO CELL PHONES sign on the wall as she pressed the CALL button. She hardened her voice. "What the fuck was that?"

The voice on the other end made her shiver. "Your friend was getting too close."

Sofia. Her throat tightened. "Where is she?"

"We took care of it."

Oh fuck. Had they killed her? Or just threatened her?

Remy's eyes burned with tears, but she wouldn't let them fall. She'd shed enough of those in her lifetime to grow a new skin, thicker this time. Sofia's old boyfriend, a soldier, had lost friends, teammates, in the line of fire—she wasn't so different. "Then why are you calling me?"

"I have another job for you."

She didn't know why Moreland called her himself. Or why he didn't bother to disguise his voice. But then, that was power. That was hubris. He didn't have anything to fear from her, and he knew it. He held all the cards.

He had her sister. *Allison, where are you?*

Her heart twisted. "No more. We agreed."

"You don't get to decide that, young lady. But if you do everything you're supposed to, this will be the last one."

She listened to his oily voice give her instructions, the last meeting before she'd get Allison back. How messed up would she be after years of abuse? But Remy couldn't think about that. She couldn't focus on anything other than getting her back.

A nurse peered around the corner, frowning when she saw the cell phone in Remy's hand. Remy put her hand over the mouthpiece. She barely cared anymore. They could all go fuck themselves. As if any of the little rules ever helped, as if they saved any lives. What Remy was doing would save her sister's life.

The nurse's lips were still pursed with annoyance. "Your friend's awake. If you want to see him."

"Yes. I do. Please. Thank you so much."

She hit END on the phone, not bothering to say goodbye, and went inside. The room was small, but at least it was private. Andre was hooked up to so many tubes, she was afraid to touch him. But when his eyelids struggled open, she recognized the same brilliant intelligence that had drawn her to him. Only then did it fully hit her, how much she loved this man and how close she'd come to losing him.

"Andre," was all she could say. Her vision blurred and finally, unstoppable, the tears fell.

"It's okay, Remy. I'm okay." He sounded surprised to see so much emotion from her. She knew he thought she didn't really care about him. Hell, she had thought so too.

"I'm sorry I was so…you know." She wiped

her cheeks. "But I'm going to make this right between us. I want us to be good. Like we should be."

His shaky laugh ended on a groan. "You're killing me here."

She took his hand, one of the few parts of him not bandaged, and laid her damp cheek against it. He cupped her face.

Pressing a kiss to the center of his palm, she said, "I just have one more thing I need to do. Then I'm all yours."

This would all be over soon. One last job.

Oh God, Sofia, I'm sorry. Remy would make this right.

She'd make Moreland pay.

CHAPTER TEN

I T WAS THE dream again.

He couldn't see much, just shadows and the occasional glint of yellow teeth and the whites of some fucker's eyes. They kept asking questions, but he couldn't hear them over the rat-tat-tat beat of his heart. He couldn't answer either, his mouth too swollen to form words. It felt full of metal, but that was only blood. His blood. He was losing too much. He'd seen enough men die to recognize his own fate.

When the bat had shattered his knee on one leg and his femur on the other, his odds of escaping had dropped to near nil. Three days of no food and little water hadn't helped. At least his team was safe. Every time their lips formed the phrase *where are they,* all he heard was *they're safe, they're safe.* He'd die with that thought, and it would be worth it.

But they weren't asking now. There were only shadows in front of his eyes, sinuous as smoke. He couldn't hear them either. Usually they talked and laughed right outside, while the stink of cheap cigarettes drifted in through the barred windows. His feet were losing circulation, tied too tight to the legs of the chair. His eyes burned; his neck ached. He waited in the quiet, wondering if they'd given up on him.

If they'd left him to a slow death. Damn.

Twigs crunching on the ground drew his attention. Guess they were back. The sound cut off as quickly as it started, like putting a shell to his ear and then pulling it away. Why would they bother with stealth in the middle of nowhere, on land they controlled?

Faint scratching came from the roof.

Unless it wasn't them.

Who would come in through the goddamn roof? His own team, come to save him. Relief poured through him, cool and sickly sweet. Jesus, he would get out of here. Even if he ended up dying in some military hospital in Germany, he'd be out of this place. Lying flat, lights low, his arteries flooded with painkillers—*yes.* It sounded like heaven.

Only, wait. How long had it been since his captors had left him? Hours? Days? It hadn't seemed that long, if he was only just now wondering about abandonment. It was a problem, because time came and went, folded over under the weight of the pain so he couldn't be sure where the creases had been.

Had his team already neutralized the threat? Or were they walking into a trap?

And he couldn't do jack shit. Just sit and wait for the scene to play out with his hands literally tied behind his back.

Light scuffs on the concrete floor came from behind him. They moved swiftly and softly. One went to the window, back against the wall, peering out. The second to the door, same position, ready to pounce. The last circled him. His commanding officer, Master Sergeant Josh Parrish. A father, a husband, a mentor—his friend.

"Hang on, buddy." Josh cut through the ropes, inadvertently digging into the cuts on his ankles.

He hadn't meant to talk, but a low groan came out anyway, an animal sound that raised the hairs on his own sweat-soaked neck.

"Sorry, man. Sorry." There was genuine remorse in Josh's voice as he worked at the ropes. He probably blamed himself for Nate's capture. But it wasn't his fault. Nate had understood when the black copter had lifted off without him. He'd played evasion games for two days before getting himself captured. He had never had any illusions about what this was. It was war, his life forfeit as soon as he'd enlisted.

In the distance, he heard a sound, a high-pitched whine. Aircraft? His team had most likely come in a copter, same as the one they'd brought in before. It would be waiting at some rendezvous point a few miles away. So why was the sound getting louder?

"No, it's a trap," he tried to yell, but it came out all in a jumble. All they saw was the tortured man flailing and screaming at them, and they thought he'd gone crazy.

"We'll get you out of here," Josh said fiercely.

Jesus, no no no. His broken mouth wouldn't form the words.

The first missile missed them, hitting some-where outside the earth and rocking the ground beneath them. The second was a direct hit. That was all that registered, the crumble of the stone wall where it stood, the pressure as Josh threw his body over Nate's. Nate couldn't move, his hands still tied and his body still broken. He could do nothing but call out hoarsely as his friends died all around him and right on top of him.

Chapter Eleven

NATE WOKE UP with a dry throat and a
pounding heart. Jesus, the dream again. His
knee pounded too, and he wondered if he was still
half-asleep, one foot in the past where his knee
was still split into two hundred parts and buried
underneath a ton of rubble.

But no, he was awake and it still hurt like hell.
Had he pulled an all-nighter, watching for some
scumbag husband to emerge from a prostitute's
hotel room? Had he stormed some terrorist cell's
shit-hole apartment looking for intel with his
team?

He shifted slightly, becoming aware of a soft
warm weight in his arms. *Sofia.*

Not back in that hellhole, not on a job. Yes,
this was what he wanted. His knee still ached with
a vengeance, but even so, he felt his muscles relax.
He could breathe again for the first time in
months, because Sofia was beside him.

He knew the feel of her, the faint scent of sex

that she wore like a perfume that drove him crazy. His fingers would smell like her, taste like her. He would have made her come and come and come, until he'd been ready to burst, and then buried himself inside. That was about how he felt right now—about to blow. Actually his erection felt painful…constricted…because he was wearing jeans.

Oh shit. Now he remembered.

He hadn't come last night. She'd been sexy…and vulnerable. So he'd gone to bed hard, which explained the extreme case of blue balls this morning.

A light sound floated in through the bedroom door. Had that woken him? He tensed. But then he heard the beep from the fancy cappuccino maker in the kitchen and figured no bad guy would be quite so ballsy. Not to mention no one could get through Josh's security system, at least without grade A explosives.

Which meant there was an emergency of another kind. The need to get Sofia out of here before Josh spotted her. The alpha wolf inside him wanted to snarl and snap.

He straightened the sheet over Sofia's leg, then stood and tugged on his T-shirt.

Sofia blinked up at him sleepily. "Come back

to bed."

That look hit him like a ton of bricks every time. Her big brown eyes framed by long lashes were enough to make any man weak at the knees, but the emotions there slayed him. Not beneath the surface, right in the open—unafraid. They made him want to do stupid things, make promises he couldn't keep. But one question always curbed that impulse: *what's a stunner like you doing with a slacker like me?* So he kept his shit to himself. No one wanted to hear it anyway, least of all himself.

The swelling on her cheek had gone down, the bruise nothing more than a faint scuff on her cheek. Just a blemish, like the first swipe of dark paint on white—at once stark and slight—and it made him burn with rage. At those faceless, nameless men for hurting her. At himself, for walking out on her so that she was alone and defenseless. And he was going to leave her again.

He turned to see Josh's tall, imposing silhouette in the doorway.

"Isn't this cozy?" he said with a smirk.

He kept his voice bland. Not possessive as hell. "You're back."

Josh looked sharp in black fatigues and combat boots even after a long night on a plane, but then, that was why he got paid the big bucks. That and his teams at North Security, which was what Nate needed to talk to him about.

He leaned against the doorjamb, the diagonal of his body more shadow than form. He ran knowing eyes over Sofia's barely covered body. "Looks like I missed the fun. I figured you had something naughty in mind when I got your call last night, but I had no idea you were bringing me a present. She's lovely."

Nate suppressed a growl and glanced back at Sofia, who was still rubbing the sleep from her eyes. She had to have been exhausted after being nearly blown up and shot at yesterday, not to mention being manhandled by him. Though she was clearly curious about Josh and hadn't missed the familiarity there. Or the innuendo. No, scratch that. Josh didn't do innuendo. Just a Mack truck of sex, and Sofia's dark bronze eyes were seeing too much—things that weren't even there, at least not anymore.

"I'll meet you in the kitchen."

He didn't care if it was rude to order Josh out of his own fucking room. He owed Nate a whole stack of favors, and Nate was going to collect on a few of them today. Besides, if he looked at Sofia with those hungry eyes for one more second, Nate was going to lose his shit.

Josh grinned, completely at east. "Don't stop on my account."

"Out."

He put up his hands in mock surrender. "I'm going, I'm going."

Once he was gone, Nate tossed Sofia's backpack onto the bed. "Take your time getting ready. I need to talk to him."

Sofia raised her eyebrows. "A present?"

He shrugged as if it didn't bother him. "He's a dick. I called to let him know we were crashing at his house."

Not waiting for a response, he left the room and gently shut the door behind him so she'd have some privacy. Josh was waiting for him with a cup of something caffeinated and potent. Nate swallowed it, embracing the scalding heat down his throat. At least it distracted him from the ache in his knee. He forced himself to walk without a limp to the table. Josh was a friend, but he wasn't the kind of person to show any weakness.

He slung himself across one of the tiny kitchen chairs. "Jesus. Did you have to stare at her like that?"

Josh gave an exaggerated sigh. "I didn't know you were possessive, Nathaniel. Why'd you bring her if you aren't going to let her play?"

He kept his expression blank. "I told you in the message. Some shit went down; we needed a safe place."

"Care to elaborate on this shit?"

Josh could be a thorn in his side, but he was damned good at operations. He was head of operations for North Security, a company he owned with his brothers. Nate was counting on that.

"Sofia works at the *Austin Daily*."

His friend's eyes sharpened. "The explosion. It's all over the news."

"Yeah. And when she went home, there were three professionals in her apartment. I took two of them out. The third is in APD custody."

His gaze flitted down to Nate's knee, but thankfully he didn't comment on it. "So, you brought her here for a little slumber party. What's the plan now?"

"I was hoping you could tell me. I want your firm to protect her."

"While you bow out gracefully?"

His smile was wry. "As gracefully as I can with a fucked-up knee. That's why I need you to do it. I'll hire you if I have to."

Josh rolled his eyes. "You know I can't take

your money after the number of times you've covered my ass." His grin widened. "In more ways than one."

Great. All he needed was Josh coming on to both him and Sofia, like a threesome was the answer to their security problem. They'd done that a few times before, when Nate was still enlisted and Josh worked for the shadow teams.

Nate set the mug down, leaning forward and looking him right in the eye, a meeting of the minds. "This is important to me."

"Hmm."

"And like you said, you owe me."

Josh looked speculative. "When's the last time anything was important to you?"

His psychobabble intuition was probably what made him good at his job. On paper he'd been a soldier—employed by the US of A, same as Nate. In reality he'd been covert ops. The kind of guy they sent in to find things out before the team went in. They'd met in Nate's first tour, Nate fresh out of training, Josh casual and mysterious. They had kicked ass in the field and gone wild when they'd had leave. Getting blackout drunk, having threesomes. It had been more than a hobby; it was a survival mechanism. A release valve for when he'd seen too many things—and done too many things.

Josh had made a respectable business with his brothers back home, but he'd never quite abandoned his party ways. And now Nate had made it worse by bringing Sofia here. Except he would rely on very few people to protect Sofia, and Josh was unfortunately at the top of the list.

"Will you take the job?" he asked.

A soft sound alerted him to Sofia coming out of the bedroom, dressed in jeans and a T-shirt. Her satin black hair was pulled behind her head in some sort of braid, but strands escaped the confines, framing her face.

She sat across from him. "Shouldn't I be consulted if I'm going to be left with strangers?"

She looked soft and pretty. Like prey. Nate knew how the world worked, how cold it could be, how harsh. Sofia would be used up, hurt, *killed*—but he wasn't going to let that happen.

"No," he answered curtly.

"I'd like to hear what she has to say," Josh drawled, a wicked glint in his eyes.

That fucker better not lay a finger on her. Nate would make that clear enough when Sofia wasn't in earshot. "You can hear what she has to say when I'm gone."

Sofia's dark eyes blazed. "Where are you going?"

She was a mix of strength and fear. Her strength was what had attracted him. Her fear was natural, considering what had happened. Which was why he'd find the fuckers who'd threatened her and put them down.

"Josh specializes in personal security. You'll be safe with him while I figure out who's behind this while you're here."

"Why can't I come with you?" Her eyes were clear, guileless. He loved that about her, but he never really knew what to do with it. Like holding a priceless vase; he could marvel at its beauty, but his first instinct was to put it out of reach, away from his clumsy hands.

He tried to explain. "I wouldn't be able to focus if you were with me—"

"Why not?"

"Yeah, Nathanial," Josh drawled. "Tell us why you can't focus when she's around."

He scowled at Josh, then turned to Sofia. "They're after you, not me. They'll be on the lookout for you."

"What are they going to say, aim for any dark-haired girl in Austin? That would be half the female population."

If she thought she didn't stand out in a crowd,

she was more naive than he'd realized. "A gorgeous young woman with a press pass from the newspaper just bombed, asking pointed questions about campaign finance reform," he corrected. "I doubt there'll be a crowd of people all doing the same thing."

"Nate." Sofia leaned forward, eyes intense, and he was startled for a minute, caught by how he must have looked to Josh just a minute ago, seeing his reflection in the woman he loved. "This is my story. I didn't give it up when a more senior reporter came sniffing around, and I'm not giving it to you either."

He was impressed…and quietly, deeply terrified. She wasn't going to quit. Her curiosity, her unquenchable sense of justice—they were going to get her killed. She would die, and he would be helpless to protect her. Like his teammates.

"This isn't up for debate," he said roughly. "You're staying here."

"You can't make me," she said. At the stubborn expression on his face, her eyebrows rose. "That's kidnapping."

"Only if you try to leave," he said reasonably.

Sofia made a frustrated sound and pushed away from the table. Josh smiled into his coffee cup, the bastard. Nate needed to figure out some way to convince Sofia to stay here. Her own safety was apparently not important enough, but to him… God, to him it was everything. She was everything. How could he let her march into a land mine? She thought he was worried about kidnapping? He didn't give a fuck about anything but keeping her safe.

He struggled for the words, which always, always failed him. He was good with his hands, in combat or in bed. But he couldn't say the things he wanted in just the right way—that was Sofia's strength. Her articles exposed corruption and shone light on people working for positive reform. She spent her time making things better, while his only skill set was tearing them down with violent efficiency. She focused on the future while he was chained to the past by a wound that would never heal.

Frustrated, he ran a hand through his hair. His cell phone buzzed on the kitchen table. He flipped it over. Tony, his computer guy. He'd prefer to take the call in another room, but aside from the fact that there almost *were* no other rooms in this cavernous house, his knee felt swollen and completely stiff.

He leaned back in the chair and closed his eyes as he answered the phone. "Yeah."

"Know any travel agents?" Tony always cut right to the point.

"Should I?"

"You've got an itinerary, real detailed. Expense reports. Pages and pages of the stuff."

Nate leaned forward. "Mexico?"

"Bingo. The scanned images of those reports were layered underneath the original images."

"What kind of knowledge would it take to pull that off?"

"This is some advanced level tech. High encryption, the kind the NSA doesn't want to admit they can't crack. That's why it took me all night."

"So we're looking at a pro."

"A pro? There's only a few people in the country who could have rigged this. But there's something else in here, an Easter egg. Looks like this was set to unlock all by itself in seventy-two hours."

"Shit. What happens in seventy-two hours?"

Sofia looked at him, dark eyes full of worry. Worry, because some shit was likely going to go down. And the person who had left this thought they might not survive.

He spoke into the phone. "Thanks, man. I owe you one."

"You know I'll collect. I'm sending you the

embedded images now." The call ended.

Both Sofia and Josh watched him expectantly. Damn, if he weren't careful, these two could end up ganging up on him. Then he wouldn't stand a chance. Though if he was honest, he realized he was already lost.

By the time he filled them in on the contents of the files, Sofia had commandeered the laptop, scanning the files with her reporter face. He wouldn't admit it, but her reporter look was the sexiest of all. He loved her bedroom eyes and her sweet smile, but when she focused on a story, she took his breath away.

Forcing his attention to the screen, he saw locations on maps in Mexico. He suspected the DEA might be interested in this, but Nate was more concerned with getting Sofia out of this mess—not pushing her deeper into it.

Sofia clicked through the maps until she found a series of sepia-toned photographs with a young Moreland standing with groups of men, shaking hands and smiling. Always the politician, even before he'd run for office.

If there'd been illicit pictures, she would have expected them to be from Mexico, doing whatever shady dealings she expected from him. Or maybe in his headquarter offices in NYC. Instead these were clearly set right here in Austin, the rolling hills behind them, the iconic 360 bridge still under construction in one of them—giving her a timeline, at least.

"You recognize any of them?" he asked her.

She shook her head, squinting. "One of them…maybe. No. Damn it, I don't know."

There were a few men in the pictures, some of them blurry, some of them already old two decades ago. One man was young, possibly younger than Moreland, with thick glasses and a striped shirt. He looked like more of a computer geek than a shady drug dealer.

Nate bent close to her. "Who uploaded these files?"

"My intern," she said absently, studying a photograph of two men, Moreland and another man in slacks and a buttoned shirt. Then she looked up. "You think he was the one who added these other images? But why would he need to hide them? Why not just put them next to the other files he uploaded?"

He just shrugged. "Someone did."

She still seemed skeptical. "He doesn't have any ties to the campaign. He goes to school full-time, works in the library, and does research for me a few hours a week. I don't see why he'd do this."

"I just had a great idea," Josh said. "Why don't you find him and ask?"

Goddamn it, *no.* He needed to keep her safe, to wrap her in layer after layer of glass and plastic and metal until no one could ever get at her, to hide her with darkness and shield her with apathy, so that no one could hurt or corrupt her—not even him.

"I'll go find him," he said, turning to Sofia. "You stay here."

"He's not going to talk to you. He doesn't know you. And like I said, it's my story. I'm going. Besides, no one will recognize me on campus."

"Actually," Josh said. "You'll blend in just fine with the students. He's the one who's going to stick out like a sore thumb. Especially with that beard. And his wild hair. I swear he looked more civilized in Macedonia."

Nate didn't know how to stop this. They were talking, but he couldn't hear a thing. This was the eerie quiet, when he wondered where everyone had gone. And later there'd be a high-pitched whine, the signal too little and too late. He might as well tie his hands behind his back too. They were going out in public. He'd do his best to protect her, but there was that chance, that horrible fucking chance that it wouldn't be enough.

Chapter Twelve

Ten years ago

AFTER THE FLOOD they had moved to Houston, where their father had found work at a construction company. Her mom had cleaned an office building downtown. They had a small apartment instead of a house, but things had been okay. Then the car accident happened.

A drunk driver. Diego had been seventeen then. Sofia, thirteen. They had gone to live with their grandmother in San Antonio, the three of them bound mostly by grief.

Diego had gotten involved with the gang early on, but he had still lived at home.

Sofia had still pretended they were a family, instead of just leftover people. Survivors.

All that changed the night that Diego went to a party, flirting with some girl from the wrong side. His own gang brothers had decided to teach him a lesson using Sofia. She tried to block out the memories, but they still came to her at night—sweaty bodies and urgent grunts and red bandannas.

She survived that too.

The sound of drunk shouts came from outside the window, making her jump. She curled up in her closet, underneath the hanging dresses and jeans, beside the tennis shoes she wore for track.

A tall silhouette filled the doorway. *Diego.*

"I can't," she said urgently, panicked. Panting. "I can't. I can't."

Silence. Then, "They won't touch you. I won't let them."

They had already touched her. He meant they couldn't touch her again, but she didn't see how that was possible. They'd been willing to hurt her even when he had been one of them. What protection would she have when he had tried to leave the gang?

There was only one way out; he knew that.

And then what would happen to her?

Some kind of blast came from the front yard. A small yelp escaped her. It wasn't a gunshot, she didn't think. But she knew they were armed. Maybe an explosion. A fire? *Oh God.*

He handed her something. Moonlight from the window glinted off the blade. "Take this."

"I can't," she repeated, praying for the numbness to come back.

"*Fucking take it.*" He ran a hand over his head. "Fuck. I'm sorry. I need you to have this. And lock your door after I leave. I already called the cops, but they may not get here in time."

He'd called the cops? That wasn't something anyone did around here. Even her grandmother had taken her to the free clinic when she'd seen her bruises. The people there had called the cops anyway, but Sofia had just shook her head. She didn't know them, couldn't recognize them. A lie, but it would keep her alive.

Except that her brother couldn't live with what had happened to her. So he'd told the gang he was leaving. Even though he still had the gang tattoos across his chest. Even though he still wore the red bandanna tucked into his jeans. You could take the boy out of the gang, but not the gang out of the boy.

For two days he'd sat around the house with a bottle of Jack in one hand, his gun in the other. Sofia hadn't known what to say to him. Abuela had pretended nothing was wrong, cooking all their favorite meals until the fridge overflowed.

Now it was midnight, and their reprieve was over.

"What are you going to do?" she asked, her voice shaking.

"I'll hold them off long enough."

She blinked, fear creeping up like rising water, drowning her. "They'll kill you."

He laughed. "How else was I going to die, hermanita? From someone else's gun. Better than mine."

Her throat clenched. "Stay here. With me."

"In the closet? They might come through the door. If it happens, I'll shoot for the biggest, toughest assholes and hope the rest will scramble like cockroaches. I don't want you near that."

Upstairs wasn't far enough away. "I'm scared."

"No matter what. They're crazy fuckers, but they aren't stupid."

Hot tears streamed down her cheeks. "You're the stupid one if you're going to go down there alone."

His voice softened. "I know, Sofia. I'm stupid and I'm crazy, but I'm your brother. This time I'm going to act like it. Lock the door behind me."

He dropped the knife on the carpet beside her. Then he turned to leave, the red bandanna in his jeans a streak of color against the dark, blurred by her tears. She watched him go, her heart a hard knot, knowing that would be the last time she saw him. And no matter what he had done before, he was a hero now.

Chapter Thirteen

Nate didn't speak to her as they drove to campus. Actually he hadn't said much since he'd come out of the bathroom looking like a different man, his beard shaved and hair trimmed short. That way he could walk around campus without standing out, Josh said.

The man must be blind.

Nate's cool blue gaze felt like a spark, sharp and hot. The rest of his six-foot, muscled body was the thunder that followed. He would never blend in. Sofia had been struck by electric lust the first time she'd seen him—digging through the trash, no less.

She'd wanted that trash.

They were both looking for a scoop, him for a client and her for the paper. The mayoral candidate that year had been hiding some serious money from his ex. They'd gotten together almost immediately and managed to track down the bank accounts.

She had broken the story and gotten all the credit; he refused to take any. He always refused. Once they'd been hanging out at his office and a client had come by to pay his balance. Personally, instead of sending a check or giving a credit card number over the phone, because he wanted to thank Nate.

You saved my marriage, the man had said.

Nate had looked pretty much the way he looked now, his eyebrows drawn low and lips set in a straight line. As bold and flat as a *Keep Out* sign tacked on a chain-link fence. She never understood why he was unhappy then, but she understood this time. He wanted her to stay behind. Stay behind while he worked on *her* story. Wasn't going to happen.

There was a time she'd been too afraid to fight her own battles, when she'd had to hide in the closet, clutching a knife. She wouldn't be that girl again. She *couldn't* be that girl, because the thought of living in that dark place made her palms sweat, her heart pound.

Some days it felt like she had escaped the chains of her past.

Other days it felt like she had one foot stuck in that closet.

He parked in a garage on the fringe of campus. "Do you have an address for this guy? A dorm number?"

"Matt works in the undergraduate library. We talked about that when he came in for the interview. It's how he knows how to access all the archives."

"You'll talk to him, and then we'll get the hell out of here."

Sofia blinked into the bright daylight as they emerged from the garage. "Don't tell me you're worried about something happening. There's a million people here."

"There were people at the *Daily*."

Her eyes closed at the reminder. *God.*

She forced herself to swallow. She needed to focus, to figure this out. It was part of the restitution to her friends. It was also the way she was going to stay alive. The explosion at her office had been suspicious. The attack by armed mercenaries at her home had been too damned close. Only Nate's timely presence had saved her. Now she had to do her part to save herself.

When she'd regained her composure, she said quietly, "They have no way of knowing I'm here."

He pulled her into the stairwell. His gaze pierced hers. "I need to tell you something. To...to make a deal with you."

His words were weighted down with something she didn't fully understand. They pulled at her, dragging her to the precipice, as if she could tumble right into his bottomless eyes. Had she ever seen him so open, almost pleading? No, never, and she couldn't deny him. It didn't matter what it was. Though he wouldn't agree, she was his.

Before he'd even saved her life, she was his.

He looked grim. "I know the odds are they don't know you're here. But still, it's a risk, and that makes me... I don't like it."

She nodded, because this much at least she understood. He was scared. Not for himself but for her. He didn't think he was a hero, but he threw himself in front of every threat. He protected her with his whole body.

"I'll be careful." She was scared too, because if something happened he would be the first to fall. Her insides felt like they were made of Jell-O, shivery and see-through.

He was just the opposite, carved in ice, the cold leaking from his skin.

"Anything could happen," he murmured. "You could be spotted. Someone could tip them off. Our best bet is to get in and out."

She waited, knowing there was more. This

was Nate on a mission, sharp and focused.

"I want you to promise me that we'll leave as soon as we talk to him. Five minutes and we're gone. Off campus and back to Josh's place or wherever the hell we go, but somewhere safe."

"Five minutes?" She could spend thirty minutes interviewing someone, hours following a lead. Days and weeks cracking open this story.

"Five minutes." His eyes were dark with urgency and frustration and something else—worry. His body tensed as if preparing for rejection. He wanted her to say yes but expected her to fight.

"Okay," she said softly.

He took a minute to process that. She heard his soft exhale—relief.

"Let's go," he muttered, leading the way outside. He walked quickly, so she could barely keep up, and she knew he was counting down the minutes before the timer had even started.

They found Matt at a deserted information desk on the second floor. They had never met in person, just exchanged e-mails, but she recognized him from his picture in the staff listings. He had a book open and headphones in. Nate fell back as they reached the landing, letting her approach on her own but staying within sight—and probably earshot too.

She rapped on the desk.

Matt looked up and then did a double take, yanking the headphones out. "You're okay."

Her heart thumped painfully. There was so much pain and fear and hope tied up in that one thought. *I'm okay.* And she wanted to stay that way.

He came around the counter, reaching out as if to embrace her. At the last minute he stopped, but she wanted that contact, the connection with her job and her friends. She stepped forward and hugged him. After a second, he squeezed back.

"Have you heard anything?" she asked, unable to voice their names: Andre. Remy.

He shook his head. "Only what they're saying on the news. They're not releasing any names yet. Some bullshit about sorting out identities and notifying the families, but I think they can't figure out what's going on themselves."

Her heart sank. "I need to talk to you about the Moreland files."

"Who's he?" He nodded to Nate, who lounged in the corner. Not relaxed—tension wound through him like a coiled spring. He saw their wariness and returned it with a bland regard.

Who was he? She wasn't sure she even knew.

Her hero. Her lover. "A friend." She turned to

Matt. "We can trust him."

After a moment's hesitation, he nodded. "What do you want to know?"

He had to be twenty or so based on his college record, not far off from her twenty-four years, but he looked young to her. His face was smooth, his torso thinner than hers. How had he gotten all tied up in this? It was only supposed to be a few hours for college credit. He'd always seemed a little immature to her, kind of goofy, but now he was solemn. Judging by his distrust of Nate, he understood the stakes.

There were two chairs behind the curved information desk, though it was clear from the deserted hallway that there was no need for two people. Probably not even one. She sat in the chair beside him, lowering her voice. "The files you uploaded the night before. Can you tell me about what was in them?"

He nodded. "The articles from his early campaigns. The campaign documents."

"Right, the documents." She tried not to sound too eager. "Where did you get them?"

He looked confused briefly. "From the FEC disclosure database. Where you told me to get them."

"Did you...add anything to the files? Any

other documents? A secret file?"

He blinked. "A what?"

Damn, probably not then. If he hadn't added those layers, who had? She pointed at the ancient-looking monitor on the desk. "Show me where you got them. Can you pull them up here?"

"Sure. It's public record."

The filed documents were public record, the ones that were vague and convoluted and missing half the cash. Instead of going to the SEC website, he logged into the school's network and pulled up his student storage drive. It was organized much like hers, separated by story. Moreland's file was at the top, the most recent, and he clicked it open.

She scanned the list of files—and their sizes. Too small. These weren't the same files that had been on the *Daily*'s servers.

She sat back. "Are you sure you didn't change these files before uploading them?"

"No. I dragged them directly from here."

"And no one was around when you did that?"

He looked worried. "There's usually a few folks around at night when I go. No one I talked to. What are you talking about, secret files?"

"Other images were embedded in the files you left there." She stopped herself from saying what exactly was in them, but he seemed to understand.

"You found it. The scoop."

Her eyes narrowed. "How did you know if you weren't the one who put it there?"

His lips pressed together. Finally, as if divulging a secret, he said, "I recognize the look in your eyes. I did work for my high school paper all four years. I know what it feels like to find a scoop, even if mine was only about the gym teacher banging the cheerleaders."

She gave him a sideways glance. "That's a pretty big scoop."

"I know." His eyes sparkled a little. He liked catching her off guard, taking her low estimation and flipping it upside down.

"Okay," she conceded, and it meant *okay, I'm sorry I didn't take you seriously; I do now.* The truth was that she barely knew him. She remembered a quick interview in Andre's office when he'd been hired. Then mostly she e-mailed him instructions and got back the research she needed the same way.

He considered her. "Besides, if you're here asking questions and you're not injured, then either you helped cause the explosion…or you know who did."

"You shouldn't be so quick to rule out the first possibility. Just because I'm a Latina doesn't mean I can't participate in a terrorist plot. Don't make assumptions."

"It wasn't because of that."

She raised her eyebrow.

"It wasn't *only* because of that." He grinned. "Also because you're pretty."

Nate snorted; she hadn't realized he'd come closer, almost behind the desk with them. "Really?" he asked. "You're going to hit on my girl while I'm in the room?"

Matt's expression of surprise rang patently false. "I thought you guys were just friends."

"I hadn't thought you were stupid. Until now." But there was no heat behind Nate's insult. Matt had clearly disarmed him as much as he had her. There was no subterfuge here…nor were there any answers. He hadn't been the one to embed those receipts.

She looked to Nate. He had taken over the mouse, clicking through a few of the files aimlessly.

He stood. "Nothing. They could have been added after the fact, while they were on the server. The question is who would have access to it."

"Anyone. Everyone who worked at the *Daily*. Our folders didn't have individual permissions like the university's drive. The real question is who knew the images would be there. Who would care?"

"Someone who wants to bring Moreland down," Nate said.

"He's the key." Only she couldn't find him.

She slid her glance to Matt, who was watching them avidly. He only knew the cover story, that she was looking into the campaign finance aspect. Surely he suspected it was more than that now, but she wasn't going to fill in the blanks. Telling him would only put him at risk. In fact, her presence here might put him at risk. No one knew she was here, but if they found out somehow…if they showed up on campus, guns blazing like they'd done at her apartment…

"We've got to go. Thanks for your help. Don't talk to anyone."

Matt looked surprised. Nate just softened. He seemed to understand her fear; he'd been trying to warn her all along. He took her hand and led her toward the stairs.

"I know how you can see Moreland."

Matt's voice came from behind them and wrapped around her throat like a vise. She stopped.

"Five minutes," Nate muttered.

She didn't move. Couldn't move. This was

the man who'd hurt her friends. "Where?"

"Right here. Well, the next building. He's giving a speech on campus tonight. Kind of a modified town hall setup where students can submit questions about the war on drugs. The event is called Building a Better Future."

Her fingers twitched, almost pulling out of Nate's hand, but he tightened his grasp. There was no question that she would go. All that remained was to convince Nate. Nate, who hated her job and the strain it put on their relationship—she could have laughed. Right now it was putting a strain on their survival.

She turned to look at him. His mouth was tense, little lines indenting the newly shaved skin around his lips. His eyes were the worst. Frustration bloomed brightly, but beneath that, at the very root, was worry. He wanted to keep her safe—was that so bad? Was that so wrong?

No. He was right. She was the wrong one.

"I'm going." Her friends. Her story. The entire sum of her life minus one Nate-shaped piece. "I have to."

Rejection didn't always come with a shove; this time, he simply let go of her hand.

"Nate." Her voice was tremulous. That was how she felt, shaky and uncertain.

He ran his hand through his hair, but there wasn't enough of it left. "I can't do this."

"Do what?" Even though she knew. He couldn't deal with her need to follow the story. He couldn't deal with her breaking her promise. He couldn't deal with *her*.

His voice was raw. "I either have to protect you or not. I can't stay…in the middle. Standing by while you put yourself in danger and then just watch it happen."

She couldn't even deny it. Confronting Moreland, even in a public setting, was dangerous. She had to do it, had to take this chance for her friends, for herself. To prove to herself that she was capable of confronting evil, not forever stuck in that closet.

But how could she ask Nate to stay?

It didn't matter. He was leaving. He was only standing in front of her, waiting for absolution before he left. Waiting for her to become a different person.

"It's okay," she said. "I understand."

She repeated the words under her breath as he turned and walked away. It was better that he was safe, away from this, but his anger sliced her open. She watched his newly trimmed head and broad shoulders leave through the tall glass windows. *I understand. I understand.*

Though she didn't, really. If he were a different sort of man, it would make more sense. But he had once trained and fought with one of the most elite forces in the world. The motto of the Army Special Forces was *To Free the Oppressed.* He had sworn to that—he'd lived it. What had changed him so much that he couldn't even understand her need to do the same?

"I'm sorry," Matt said. He seemed really upset, genuinely remorseful. "I didn't think he'd leave."

"No, I'm glad you told me. He's just…" Hurt. She'd hurt him.

"Pretty intense. I really didn't mean to make him mad."

"He'll be fine." *He left. He left. He left.* "So tell me about this town hall speech."

Matt filled her in on the campus chatter about the speech, and she pretended to listen. Damn it, this was important. But he'd left. Should she have listened to him? Gone after him?

It was too late to change her mind now. Had he gone back to Josh?

She had half a mind to drive up there. No idea how to find his house, but still.

Matt's voice cut into her thoughts. "So, does

that sound like a good plan?"

She blanked. "What plan?"

"Going down to the rec center. Some friends are meeting up there." He pressed his lips together, apologetic and a little embarrassed. "Or we could go somewhere else, if you wanted."

"No, that's okay," she assured him. "I should get back."

She extricated herself before it got even more awkward, moving along the shelves, gaze turned towards the tall windows. The sunlit courtyard outside the library somehow looked sinister without Nate. Shadows shifted in the corner of her eye, around a shelf of books.

Her heart skipped a beat. Was someone following her?

Chapter Fourteen

A HAND ON her wrist. Her breath caught. She whirled to face Nate.

"You didn't leave," she said, trying to hide her relief.

The look he gave her was reproachful. "Of course not. I'm taking you back to Josh's place. And that's where you'll stay until whoever set that explosion, whoever *really* set it, is behind bars."

Or dead. That was the implied alternate in his tone.

"I can't," she said.

"You are."

"He's speaking *tonight*. I won't get another chance like this."

He scowled. "Absolutely not."

"I never got a chance to meet him," she said. "To ask him a question and look him in the eye while he answers. This is my chance to do that, to finally know for sure if he's guilty."

"He's a politician, Sofia. A professional liar."

"I'll know if he's telling the truth about this. You can be there too, to read his body language and tell me if I'm right. I know you have experience with interrogations."

He flinched, but it was gone so quickly she couldn't be sure. His face was impassive again, soldier at the ready. "It's dangerous," he said flatly.

"All I did was go to work, and it was dangerous. I went home, and it was dangerous. If I'm going to die anyway, I might as well fight first. Do something I believe in and—"

Whatever she was about to say tumbled into his mouth as a moan. His lips had captured hers, his body holding her up against a shelf, the cool metal slats pressing into her. She resisted for a moment, pure shock and a small amount of indignation holding her stiff. But his tongue stroked hers in the same rhythm his fingers and his cock had used on her so many times. Her hands found his hair, tightening and tugging with nowhere to go.

He pulled back only long enough to say, "Don't even talk about that. You're not going to die. Over my dead body. And you're not going to see Moreland tonight."

Exactly what she was worried about, but he

was kissing her again, forcing her to forget all the practical, fearful reasons why she didn't want him involved. Instead she felt his tongue teasing hers, his hands roaming over her ass, and a hard cleft pushing up against her core.

She tore her mouth away to suck in a breath. "God," she cried. "Oh God."

"Yeah." He pushed her into an empty room, leaving the light off. It was so wrong like this, rushed and dirty in a study room where they didn't even belong, but the frantic hands and panting breaths were just right. She needed to know he was as crazy about her as she was about him. She needed to know that the King of the Slackers was a facade but this—this was real.

She tried to buck against him but only succeeded in knocking against the door.

"Shh, someone will hear," he muttered and then tugged her jeans down her legs. And then pushed two blunt fingers into her wet heat and searched and probed until he found the sensitive bundle of nerves.

She moaned, and she couldn't keep quiet.

He latched his mouth over hers and stumbled, taking her with them. He fell back on the couch, catching the brunt of their fall together. With his hands on her hips, he centered her over him, settling the ridge of his cock against her wet, pulsing sex. She gasped at the contact of his rough jeans on her sensitive clit. It was too much; she needed to get away. Except when he held her down with both hands and thrust upward with his hips—more pressure and ahhh, just right.

And still, she pulled away from the pleasure.

It scared her, how much she craved it. How much she needed it.

"What's wrong, gorgeous?" he murmured, lids low with arousal.

"I don't…" she whispered. "Tell me what to do." *Make me, make me.*

His lips firmed. "Oh, gorgeous. There's so much pain inside you."

All the pain centered at her core, where she had been violated, lost. Where she had been found again. Her knees barely brushed against the rough fabric of the sofa. She was suspended on top of him, riding the waves and helpless against its whims.

"You don't need me to hurt you," he said roughly.

"Yes," she gasped. "Do it."

Her past always crept up on her in these moments, strangling her pain, tainting her pleasure. Her brother had given his life for her, but she'd never really be free. Nate was a hero, but even he couldn't save her.

He did the opposite of what she wanted, letting his hands fall back. "You hurt enough already. More than you ever should have. Give it to me. Hurt me instead. Dig your nails into me. Mark me, gorgeous. Fucking scar me."

Impossibly she found herself obeying him, reaching for him. Her hands and mouth were touching him, grasping him, but it wasn't enough. She wanted to feel every part of him, to feel the *core* of him, and he was seated just perfectly.

She palmed his heat through his jeans, clumsy and harsh. He loved it, groaning against her lips. With a few flicks of the zipper, she pulled him into her palm, stroking the velvety shaft and swirling her thumb through the wetness at the tip. Hard, like he wanted. Rough, like she wanted.

He bucked against her with an urgency that made her hot. It was a warning: soon, no time left. This had to be more than a handjob—she owed him that—so she sank down to the floor between his knees.

"Fuck." His words came in staccato bursts of breath as he hauled her back up. "Need to be inside you. That gorgeous little pussy is all wet for me, isn't it? So fucking hungry."

He paused with the tip of his cock nudging at her entrance, her legs spread over his thighs.

His eyes were glazed with lust. "Sofia?"

She sank down around him, her eyes falling shut. "Yeah," she breathed. Though she didn't really understand the question, she knew the answer. Whatever he wanted—yes. Could she please him, keep him this time? God, she would try.

Her body slackened by the pleasure of being filled, she set up a languorous pace, a roll of her hips combined with a swivel down. It was the last part that made his breath catch, and in a matter of minutes, his thighs were trembling beneath hers.

His cock was always so impossibly hot. The first time she had touched him, she'd thought he felt feverish. But it was a sex fever, the sweetest delirium that made him call out her name. He let her rock over him until he reached his breaking point; then he grasped her hips and thrust up to meet her.

Her mouth opened on a gasp and caught there, frozen with the sharp sensation. He reached someplace inside her that twinged as the soft head of his cock breached it. She shuddered every time, unable to tell the difference between good or bad, pleasure or pain—there was only Nate. His cock filling her up. His mouth enclosing her nipple.

Her body was entwined with his, and they moved in a rhythm too intimate to name. It was a language for bodies alone, the rasp of his tongue against her pebbled nipple, the slippery scratch of his hair against her thick clit, the clenching and pulsing inside her as she came and then he did. She rode out the final notes before collapsing on him. He stretched out the orgasm, pumping again once, twice into her before his cock slipped out of her and she felt a final spurt of hot liquid against her thigh.

Sated, she remained over him in a sensual sprawl. A soft thunk shuddered through his body as his head hit the wall behind him.

"You're going to kill me." His low baritone had been run through a shredder, sliced apart and missing pieces.

Sex, he meant. Or maybe their relationship.

That was what he meant, but still she shivered at his words, as if they were a premonition. She *could* really kill him. His involvement in this mess would only lead to him being injured or worse, and Jesus, now she understood why he'd gotten so damn upset when she'd talked about dying. It made her crazy to think of him at risk. She had always wanted him to care more, like he must have in Special Forces, except that job was rife with danger. A private investigator was one of the safest jobs he could have. She understood, suddenly, the appeal of the laid-back attitude. Don't care; don't bother. Don't get hurt; don't watch your loved ones get hurt.

Lifting her head, she took in his lowered lids, his flushed lips.

"You can go," she said quietly. "I mean it. This isn't a guilt trip or some kind of trick. This isn't your fight."

Despite his disheveled state, his voice was even. Steady as a rock. "It is my fight. I should have stayed and fought for you. Not just now at the library. Back then, when you wanted me to get off my ass and do something with my life."

Guilt turned her stomach. "It wasn't my place."

"No." He put a finger over her lips. "You need to do this. I understand that."

Her throat tightened. She had wanted him to step up, and he had. "You'll let me go see Moreland?"

His expression became grim. "With me, Sofia. Always with me."

"But—"

"You have to do this, and I have to stand beside you. You have to trust me to do that."

She nodded, knowing that protection was part of him. He was a hero, whether he admitted it or not. She wondered how long that promise extended. Only while she was in danger? Only while Moreland was a threat? He'd let her walk away once before. She wasn't sure she wanted to leave again.

Chapter Fifteen

Matt slung himself into the small chair, spinning a few times before settling his elbows on the desk. So that was Sofia Mendoza. She looked younger than he'd thought. Prettier too. The pulled-back hair and small smile in her staff photo painted a different picture—more ambitious, less kind.

It had been weird working for a person he hadn't met, but those were the dues to be paid. A campus interview with a tired recruiter confirmed he had a brain between his ears. Then a quick tour of the *Daily*'s offices to sign the internship paperwork, but Sofia had been out on an assignment. So he'd put his hours in at night when he wasn't at school or working in the library or at the university newspaper, hoping to get noticed.

Not like this, though.

His mom had freaked when she saw the news. The cell phone towers in Austin were jammed for hours the afternoon of the explosion. She was in tears by the time his phone actually rang. It had taken thirty minutes to calm her down and another hour to convince her he wasn't going to drop out midsemester and fly home.

Then Sofia showing up at his work…it had thrown him. He still felt bad for lying to her. He glanced at the alarm clock. Eight o'clock. She would be at the speech right now. He had time to catch her and confess, but how well would that go over? *I think my girlfriend might have been the one to doctor up those files. Oh, and she's not really my girlfriend. I'm just kind of in love, but I don't even know how to find her.*

He'd broken his confidentiality agreement and his credibility as a reporter for what? All so he could get laid. He really hadn't meant it that way, but he had to admit, that's what he'd wanted. Though the sex hadn't happened.

Maybe she hadn't been the one to tell. He couldn't imagine *why* she had.

If she had information, why not just tell him?

Something stirred behind the door. He turned to see something small and brown dart across the floor.

"Goddamn it, Jimmy."

He followed the gerbil into the closet, but the

rodent was safely hidden under the mountain of dirty laundry. The girls in a room next door kept the gerbil in a cage, even though they weren't supposed to. Matt privately agreed with the rule for precisely this reason.

Whenever the gerbil got loose, which it inevitably did, it took days to catch him. One time he'd found Jimmy when he'd been tidying up. The days-old Cheetos bag on the floor had been heavier than it should—and wriggly. He still had nightmares about that.

"Hey."

The low voice came from behind him, and he whirled. "Shit. You scared me."

There she was, her blonde hair in a braid, her hands shoved into her jeans pockets. She smiled uncertainly, the effect less brilliant than usual but somehow more poignant. He knew he'd been stupid as to show her his work and share details, but damn. When she looked at him that way, like the whole world was in front of her, he felt something open up inside him.

He loosened, and the freedom in that was almost better than sex.

Almost, because he still really wanted to have sex with her.

"I worried about you," she said.

For a minute he wasn't sure what she meant. Of course she knew about his job at the *Daily* because he'd told her about it. Bragged, actually. "Oh, the newspaper. Yeah, I wasn't there. It's really tragic though. I've been watching it on TV."

She made this strange little shrug, almost fatalistic, stepping over the shambles of the room to the thin, clear window. Something was off about her. Every day she looked brand-new—different clothes, different hair. The same soul-tugging eyes. But today the change was more palpable. Melancholy shrouded her. He wanted to rip it away and find out what would make her smile, laugh. Did she ever laugh?

He took one step toward her. "I need to talk to you about that. Did you... That day you looked at those articles and pictures. Did you change them? Add something to them?"

She turned back sharply. The look in her eyes was soft, though. "Why would I do that?"

"There was some information on them, in back of the documents. I didn't add them so I thought maybe...maybe you did."

A sigh. "That was a mistake."

"So you *did* change the files?" He shook his head, mystified. This was like some kind of conspiracy-theory level shit. It was almost exciting to be a part of it, but he didn't understand. "Why?"

She looked away. "I wanted to help her. But I can't."

More puzzles. "Why didn't you send them to the *Daily* yourself?"

"He'd know it was me," she said flatly. "I guess he already did."

"Who?"

"I have to go."

"Wait, we need to find Sofia. We have to tell her—"

Her gaze sharpened. "Sofia is alive?"

The skin on his neck prickled. Had he told her his boss's name? Was it listed on some org chart on the *Daily*'s website? Obviously she knew more than she was telling him. She must have sought him out because of his internship at the *Daily*. That stung his ego, but then he'd always known she was too good for him.

"She came by earlier," he said.

"Where is she?"

"Probably long gone by now." A lie, but he couldn't be sure she was on Sofia's side.

"Oh." She seemed to lose interest then, glancing instead to his rumpled bed.

Of course he knew it was a distraction. She'd never had sex with him before. Hinted, yes. Made him lust after her, dream about her. But she'd never touched him.

Stepping forward, she reached her arms around his neck.

What if he was imagining things? Maybe she hadn't done anything wrong.

Or maybe he was just thinking with his dick.

He let his hands fall on her waist, eager to feel her slender form, comforted by her warmth. He'd been chilled ever since hearing the news, but her mouth on his and her knowing hands on his body was just the balm he needed.

They fell back onto the bed, her body small beneath his. She paused, blinking up at him. Tragic eyes, he thought, and then mocked himself. He should have been a poet, not a reporter.

"I didn't mean to hurt you," she whispered.

He froze, because this was their thing. The first thing she'd ever said to him was *I didn't mean to hurt you* as she'd dropped a book on his head in the library.

She hadn't hurt him this time.

In fact, he couldn't really feel anything.

Only when he looked sideways did he realize

why. The needle in her hand. He'd been too fucking horny to even register the prick.

His gaze found her face again. Tragic eyes. Regretful, guilty eyes.

He found his voice, hoarse and thready. "Why?"

She pressed her lips to his, soft and chaste. "They want me to kill you, but I won't do that. I'll keep you safe."

He fell onto his side, and the world went black.

Chapter Sixteen

ANTICIPATION AND A packed auditorium raised the temperature backstage. From the shadows, Nate watched the sound and lighting people check and recheck the systems. They had already scoped out the shitty little greenroom where Moreland should be.

His heart rate was steady, breathing even and deep. His body recognized this as a mission. He was one man instead of a team, but he took this as seriously as any mandated operation, because Sofia was here.

"You ready?" he murmured.

Her hand shook slightly as she curled her hair behind her ear. "I'm good."

She wasn't good, but he wasn't going to argue with her. He had one job, and one job only—to make sure that she stayed alive. The thought of her hurt made him rip and bulge into some sort of Hulk, but that wasn't safe. No, safest for her was the analytical intellect, the strategist, the soldier.

The exits were mapped—in his head anyway. His not-exactly-legal concealed handgun was in one boot, his KA-BAR in the other. There were plenty of unknowns, but they all factored into the equation that only had one possible outcome: they'd both get out safely.

Except whatever weapons came at them, Sofia had that hardest fight. She had to get that slimey politician to give up a secret, a lead—something. And she was nervous. He could feel her worry shimmer in the air around them.

Older, more experienced reporters had tried to penetrate the Moreland wall. They had failed. But he believed in her. "You'll get him."

She gave him a sideways glance. "How can you sound so sure?"

"Because this is what you were born to do."

To push, to fight. To put herself in danger, if that meant protecting someone else. It was what he loved and hated about her. It was the reason he'd let her walk away that first time, but he didn't think he could do it again.

✧　✧　✧

SOFIA'S EYES SCANNED the crowds. "Where is he?"

Moreland still hadn't shown up and the speech was scheduled to start in minutes.

"He'll come." Nate sounded sure, but what if the whole explosion and resultant press storm had him spooked? He might blow off the speech.

"He could be halfway to Mexico right now on another shady aide mission."

"That's the thing about egomaniacal assholes," Nate murmured. "They think they're above the law. He won't get spooked. He'll come."

Even the event organizers were starting to sweat as the minute hand leaned into the twelve. A sudden clatter from the hallway behind the stage sharpened her attention.

With three minutes to spare, Moreland arrived. Flanked on both sides by suited men, bodyguards and advisors both, he radiated geniality and confidence.

Her stomach turned over.

"And I said to him, 'Governor, how can we expect these kids to be on time to class if I don't make it to my own speech?'"

Nervous laughter met his question.

They couldn't be falling for this self-aggrandizing, name-dropping bastard, could they? But they were. Everyone backstage had frozen in place, wax statues of awe and admiration, as a female aide powdered his nose and straightened his tie.

His salt-and-pepper hair and grave brown eyes were striking, that was for sure. Sofia could see how they might be handsome if she had passed him on the street, without knowing about the invisible blood staining his hands. Blood of her colleagues. Blood of her friends.

Nate's hands were on her upper arms, restraining her. Confused, she glanced back.

His face was dark. "Not like this."

A whimper escaped her, part fear, part frustration. She fought him—stubbornness and determination filling her with a strength equal to his. And then his hands tightened on her arms, almost bruising. His brown eyes sparked with heat.

Then his hold didn't feel confining as much as protective.

She let her body fall against him, and he caught her in a tight embrace.

"Shhh," he soothed. "You'll get your interview."

She gave him a wry smile. "Reporters, always angling for the interview."

His eyes filled with something almost soft. Affection? Love? He brushed his thumb over her bottom lip. "Not you, Sofia. You were always in it for the right reasons, always willing to fight for people who needed it. I didn't stand a chance around you."

Warmth suffused her cheeks, and she looked away, uncertain. They'd done this once before, and it had nearly broken her to lose him then. Could she survive it a second time?

Her gaze turned to the backstage, filled with lights and other equipment.

And two stone-faced guards watching the crowd while Moreland spoke.

"How will we talk to him?" she asked, cursing herself for a coward. She should have been able to look Nate in the eye, to tell him she wanted him. Tell him she loved him. The fact that she couldn't said more about her fear of intimacy than it ever did about his profession, his heroism. She'd wanted to leave her childhood in the past, but it was following her around with this story.

Or maybe she was the one who couldn't let it go.

When she chanced a glance at Nate, he still had that gentle look in his eyes. "We'll be waiting for him."

Then his head lowered. His mouth touched hers, and she lost all sense of time and place. She wasn't backstage, desperate for answers, on the run for her life. She was only heat and sensation, the sum of parts that touched Nate—her mouth, her hands. Her breasts.

He backed her up against the wall, and she stumbled over thick cables. He steadied her until she leaned back, opening to him. He was a drug, *her* drug, and she felt her limbs go lax with every inhale.

Suddenly, he was gone. His hand caught hers.

Awareness returned in bright flashes of light. Applause. Cheering.

The guards had stepped onto the stage now, still off to the side but flanking Moreland. Which meant they weren't watching backstage. Nate caught her hand, and they dashed into a green-room in the back. He shut the door behind them.

"Did they see us?" she asked, breathless.

"I doubt it," he said, pushing her deeper into the room, half-hidden by a rack of suits. "He wouldn't still be talking if they suspected anything."

She touched her lips, which still tingled. "Is that why you kissed me? To make them think we were two horny college kids?"

His lids lowered. "I kissed you because I wanted to."

Heat raced through her veins. "He might not

come back here."

Nate glanced at the lighted vanity and the spread of fruit and cheese. They weren't exactly Hollywood, but the university could draw big-name speakers. "He likes to think of himself as a celebrity. He'll come."

She twisted her hands together, then forced them to her side. She was a reporter for the *Daily*, an award-winning newspaper. And this was the story of a lifetime. She'd felt that from the first time she looked at Moreland.

Maybe only someone with her past would have been that suspicious.

A deep breath. Maybe this story had always been meant for her. "So we wait."

CHAPTER SEVENTEEN

THE LOOK OF surprise on Moreland's face was gratifying.

The guns that his thugs pointed at them, less so.

Nate stepped in front of her smoothly, palms up. *Unarmed.* "Gentlemen," he said, that good-old-boy twang thicker than usual. "We don't want any trouble."

"I just have questions," Sofia added, pleased that her voice didn't shake.

Moreland's shrewd eyes took them in quickly. He nodded to the men who looked more like thugs in suits than an official security detail. "I don't think these two are any threat to me."

She lifted her chin and stepped beside Nate as the thugs reluctantly shut them inside. "Senator Moreland, I'm Sofia Reyes with the *Daily*. Do you mind if we record this conversation?"

"The *Daily*. I heard about the unfortunate events, of course." He gave her body a slow perusal. "Glad to see you made it out fine."

She felt Nate tense beside her. He wouldn't like any man checking her out, but Moreland's gaze felt especially slimy. She gave private thanks that he stayed silent, letting her run the interview. She was grateful for that.

And she was grateful that he was here. His presence gave her strength.

"I must object to the recording," the senator said with a genial smile. "This isn't a formal interview, after all."

Reluctantly she nodded and tucked the recorder in her pocket. She would play by the rules even if he didn't. "Senator Moreland, you spend a great deal of your travel time in Mexico. Is there a reason for that focus?"

His smile didn't slip. "We share almost two thousand miles with the country. Of course our relationship is important to our well-being as a nation."

A very nice sound bite. "But your stance on immigration has been strict. In fact your opponent described it as extreme."

"Good fences make good neighbors. Mexico is a beautiful nation, but they're suffering from a variety of social issues." His beady eyes didn't break contact with hers. "Drugs. Prostitution.

Violence."

Her breath caught at the warning in his words. He was threatening them, even while his words could be printed and look like a concerned politician. Fear rose up in her chest, but anger too. This was what she'd become a reporter to fight, the kind of corruption she had once seen at the lowest level. And he was the top.

It was time to stop playing nice. And the truth was, one of the male reporters at the *Daily* would have opened with this line of questioning. "Is that why you visit Mexico every other month? To confirm that prostitution and violence are still present?"

A flash of rage ripped across his face. "Young lady, you have no idea what you're stepping into."

"My newspaper was bombed for the data we had. Data about your trips. Whatever this is, I'm already deep. I'm already a part of this, and I'm not going to let it go."

His eyes narrowed; then suddenly he relaxed. His moods changed quickly, from screaming in anger to smiling at his supporters. That was part of what made him so dangerous.

Now he turned to Nate and gave a genial smile. "You look military."

"Special Forces," Nate said, his voice taut.

"Then you've seen what it's like in these third-world countries. The poverty. The danger. It's no place for a woman to visit."

Her teeth ground together at the blatant sexism, but she was gratified by Nate's terse reply.

"Women already live there."

Moreland leaned back, looking pissed. "So they do. And I do whatever I can to help. There are limitations, of course. My first priority is to my country."

"Help?" she asked softly. "Is that what you call it? You've been documented with ties to Antonio Lopez, a known cartel leader."

His expression turned pinched. "Those photos were taken a long time ago. And I met with him to see if I could convince him to stop. You go public, that's what I'll say."

And that was what he'd say about the hidden photos, the ones that showed him with men in Austin. Of course, she hadn't figured out what they proved. Something bad or he wouldn't have been willing to kill. Something bad enough that he wouldn't be so sure he could convince everyone with his denials alone. She needed to figure out what they meant.

She wouldn't find that in the greenroom of the auditorium, but she might get something. A clue. A damned lead. Her chances were better now that he was riled up. "Senator, even speculation can derail a presidential campaign."

"I have not confirmed nor denied my candidacy," he spat at her, the words practiced.

She had expected that, but she hoped he wasn't expecting this. "Won't you miss your hillside mansion if you have to live in the White House?"

His nostrils flared. "What do you know about that?"

"It's under an umbrella corporation, but I traced it back to you. It looked like a beautiful place on Google Earth, but I'm not sure why you're keeping it a secret." She paused, then went for the kill. "Or, for that matter, the warehouses in East Austin."

The pause felt thick with his anger, an animal backed into a corner.

"My privacy is extremely important to me," he finally said, his voice low. "My private investments are none of your business." He turned to Nate again. "Maybe you should keep an eye out for your girl. Like she said, she's already in deep. I wouldn't want anything to happen to her. I wouldn't want her to end up as one of my…investments."

The threat couldn't have been more blatant if he'd spelled it out in neon letters. Nate made a low growling sound. "She'll be fine. I'll make sure of it."

Sofia could feel him holding himself back, and she prayed he'd keep it in. The guards outside would shoot first and ask questions later if Moreland ended up hurt.

"You do that," Moreland said, his words oily. He snapped his fingers, and the guards stepped inside. "Show these two out."

One of the guards started to reach for them, but Nate smoothly stepped in front of her. Whatever the guard saw in Nate's eyes, he chose to step aside.

CHAPTER EIGHTEEN

THEY MADE IT outside the building, Nate tense beside her. He had always been careful with her, always made sure to stand closer to the street when they walked together, always silently swept a room before they entered it. And that had been before the bomb. It made sense that he would be more careful now, but she felt something more.

Maybe it wasn't even Nate. Maybe it was in the air around them, the crackle of danger that she hadn't been able to register outside the *Daily*'s office that day.

"Nate," she murmured, her voice shaky.

He grabbed her hand and sped up, moving them along the shadows of the large auditorium. "Exiting to the north," he said.

She blinked, struggling to keep up with his long strides. "What?"

He glanced back at her. "Almost there."

Only then did she realize he was speaking into

some kind of communication device. Had he been wearing it the entire time? Then their conversation probably had been recorded after all. Moreland had been careful enough with his words that it wouldn't matter.

"Two minutes to the meeting place," Nate said.

The urgency in his voice made her breath catch. This was more than being careful. He thought something would happen. And then something *was* happening.

All she heard was a pop. A gun? Another explosion?

Then a rush of sound, and she realized it was a car zooming by them. She barely had time to register that before Nate pressed her flat against the brick. She saw a flash of glass, of a smooth metal barrel, and then the bullets came.

Nate was shouting something. Pieces of brick pinged into her hair.

"What's happening?" she managed to say in a rush of breath.

"Moreland," Nate said shortly.

It shouldn't have surprised her, but it felt like a shock. It was one thing to know he was dirty, to suspect him, and to feel the whiz of bullets by her ears. "Why?" she said numbly. "We didn't get anything."

"Doesn't fucking matter," he muttered, pushing away from her body, moving them deeper into the shadows. "We're digging and that's enough for him to get rid of us."

Get rid of them. She swallowed hard. There was fear there, for herself. More than that she felt fear for him. What had she gotten him into?

Nate pressed a hand to his ear, listening. When he turned to her, his expression was grave. "Our backup is pinned down. We have to cross this green to the east."

She understood that if there were any other way, he would suggest it. If he believed this was their only route of escape, then it was. Even if that meant running right into the cross fire.

"On your mark," she said, her voice only a little wavery.

He nodded. "Whatever happens, don't fucking stop."

He meant if he got shot, she could keep running. She'd never leave him behind like that, but she didn't bother arguing. She just nodded, because the sooner they ran, the sooner they'd get across.

His gaze took in her features as if memorizing her. "I never should have let you leave."

Her mouth opened in surprise. Before she could form a response, he took off running, pulling her behind him. She stumbled first and then found her footing. Spongy grass sank beneath her feet.

They made it halfway across the green before the shots came again. Clumps of mud shot up at her almost as fast as the bullets, and she twisted her ankle. The ground padded her fall, but she still felt the impact in her brain, her vision a whir of lights against darkness.

She heard Nate swear. Then his hand was lifting her. The world turned upside down, a firm shoulder beneath her stomach. They were moving again. Running?

He was carrying her. *No, his knee.* It was too much for him to run, for him to support her weight as well as his, but he hadn't asked. He'd just acted like the hero that he was.

Impossibly he moved so much faster, even with a permanently injured knee, even with her weight, than she'd been able to run behind him. Dark blades of grass blended together in a long glistening streak.

Then they were on pavement again. She felt it in the burst of speed.

A car door opened.

She barely had time to register the world turning right-side up again before she was pressed into the backseat. Nate murmured to someone. Directions? Orders?

Then the vehicle jolted forward, pulling away from the bullets, from the men out to get them.

"We clear?" Nate murmured, and she knew he was still talking to someone else.

She didn't hear the response, but she felt it in the relaxation of his body.

Her hands were shaking. Her whole body was shaking. "How can he just—At a university!"

"I know, gorgeous," he said, running his hands along her arms, warming her up. "He's a fucking maniac. Are you okay? Are you hurt?"

He didn't wait for her to answer. Instead he felt along her ribs, her hips, her legs. Making sure that she was still in one piece, because God, she didn't feel like it.

"You knew, didn't you?" she asked. "That's why you didn't want me to come. You knew what he'd try."

"I suspected. If he was as dirty as you thought he was, if he knew you were digging, he'd be desperate enough for this."

"He's escalating," she said, a strange numbness creeping through her. The explosion had been huge, but easily explained as a terrorist attack. Lots of different factions and people would be interested in waging retaliation against the *Daily*. A newspaper wasn't worth its salt if it didn't make enemies. People had been injured, but no one killed, thank God.

But the people shooting at them, there'd been no terrorist group to blame, no excuse for a dead reporter. Everyone would know that whatever her story, she'd been the target. And still he'd attempted to have her killed. Was he that smug that he'd never be caught? Or was he just insane?

"If you get a clear shot, take it," Nate said as he pulled an earpiece out. "I'm going dark."

She narrowed her eyes at the easy way he operated. Of course she knew he'd been in the military. She'd had no doubt that he'd been incredibly competent and, yes, dangerous. This felt like more than old habits, though. This felt fresh.

She had known this man before. At least she thought she had.

Now she stared at him through fresh eyes, realizing things he'd never told her.

"You never left, did you?" she breathed.

He gave her a glance, a little wary. "What?"

"You're in black ops," she said, accusing.

"With Josh, I bet."

He turned and looked out the window, at nothing but black. No answer. That meant yes.

"Why? Why didn't you tell me?" she demanded.

"Why put you in danger?" he said as if this wasn't a revelation. As if this didn't change everything. "The PI thing is a cover, and it was better that you believed it."

She still couldn't believe he'd kept this a secret from her. And she couldn't believe that she, a reporter, hadn't figured it out before now. But then, he was damn good at his job. And she had been blinded by love.

Shock still resounded inside her, coloring everything he'd ever said or did. Every moment he came to her late at night, slipping into her bed when she was already sleeping. Every bruise and cut he'd ever gotten while they had been together. "Why a PI?" she asked because it was all she could manage.

A large shoulder lifted. "It lets me snoop around, ask questions, go into places I'm not supposed to be. People find out I'm a PI, they assume I'm there to dig up dirt on a cheating wife. That's familiar to them. Safe, even. Unless they're the wife."

She didn't laugh. "So all this time," she said

slowly, "none of it was real?"

In the dark interior of the car, she couldn't see his expression, but she could feel the gravity. "I did real jobs. That's how the cover stays solid. A few angry husbands and wives coming to my offices, a money trail, keeps it legit."

"And the rest of the time?"

"The rest of the time I was working with Josh."

She turned away, staring blankly out the window. Feeling more alone than she had even after the blast.

A soft touch on her arm. "Hey," he said gently. "You were wrong about one thing. Everything with you was real, Sofia. If you believe anything, believe that."

She stared at his shadowed profile, not sure whether she could trust him. Not sure that she could trust the feelings inside her—the respect for what he did, the fear that he would be hurt. The love that surged up even stronger.

"You were wrong about one thing too," she finally said.

"What's that?"

"Moreland did give us something. He told us what he's shipping." *I wouldn't want her to end up as one of my…investments.* "Women."

Chapter Nineteen

Sofia thought they'd go back to Josh's house, but instead they checked into a low-rent motel in the west side using a fake ID and cash. She wouldn't have looked twice at the fake IDs. She'd known he would have them as a private detective.

She would have looked twice at the bag of military-grade guns and other supplies. Because she hadn't known that he was working with Josh in black ops. Still a soldier, after all.

The place smelled musky, but it was clean enough.

She stared into the darkness, listening to the sound of running water. She imagined rivulets running over dusky skin and hard-packed muscle. Heat speared through her—and worry too. Years of being in the army had made Nate ruthlessly efficient. He could soap up and rinse off in a matter of minutes, so the fact that he'd been in there for half an hour was telling.

It meant his knee was hurting him.

She'd been tempted to go in with him, to run her hands along his slick skin, to get on her knees and make him forget his pain. But he wouldn't like her seeing him this way. Hurt. Weak. At least that was how he'd see it. The truth was, he was incredibly strong.

God, how could he not be hurting? He'd held her in his arms. He'd run with her. She might be slender, but she was a grown woman. And his knee had never healed fully—would never heal fully considering it had been shattered and left to fester for days before he got free. It was a miracle he could walk.

It was a miracle he was even alive.

And he'd almost died today. Because of her. Because of the work she loved so much. It had been her dream as a child, to expose the injustices she saw around her, to shine light into the darkness.

Except Nate *was* her light in the darkness. How could she risk him?

How could she give him up?

The fact that he was black ops didn't change the fact that he could die. She'd already known he could defend himself, but could he defend her against an army? The faucet squeaked as the water stopped. Nate's shadow blocked the light as he dried off his tall, broad body. The sliver of light went black.

The door opened. She felt more than saw him move across the room. Stiff. Slow.

Metal springs creaked as he slid into bed beside her. *Naked.*

It was impossible for her not to know he hadn't put on clothes. He wouldn't have had any that were clean. And she could feel the heat of him emanating beneath the sheet. And still, he didn't reach for her. Did he think she was asleep? Did he want to keep his pain a secret, even now, in the dark?

Part of her wanted to give him that space, but the pull was too strong. Too acute.

Her body moved without her knowledge, covering the distance between them, moving her palms to his furred chest. In the light he had tattoos that proclaimed his love for his country—his love for her. In the dark he was purely man—soft skin over hard muscle, gentle movement as he breathed.

"Sofia," he muttered, a warning.

Except after what they had been through, she felt like being reckless. Her lips met the indent beneath his shoulder, in that place where his muscle crested. "Nate."

A shudder ran through his body. "You could have died today."

Her heart clenched, because she knew what he wanted.

And she knew she couldn't give it to him.

When she had first met him, she'd still been a junior reporter at the *Daily*. Bright-eyed and bushy-tailed no matter how many crap assignments Andre had given her. He'd given her some page-filler assignment on the groundbreaking ceremony for Dawson Tech's new building. She was supposed to write about how great Dawson was, about the glossy building design, about the fancy ultra-natural landscaping.

Fuck him, Nate had said in that Southern drawl he got when he was extra pissed. *Give him two fucking sentences about the new building, then write whatever the fuck you want.*

That's what she'd done, using the groundbreaking as a springboard to a think piece on sexism in the booming Austin tech industry. She'd held her breath with Remy, waiting to hear what Andre was going to say.

He hadn't called her into his office that time. He'd come out with a printout of her article, copyedited in red pen—he was old-school that way. And he'd said, *You aren't fired, Mendez. Just make sure this happens again.*

"Do you remember the groundbreaking article?" she murmured.

He made a coarse sound. "I remember the other news outlets picking up your story like it was their fucking idea."

She laughed silently. He was so protective of her. And she loved that about him.

Only then did she remember, a flash of light in the dark, where she had seen the man in the picture on that hidden file. The one that had been worth blowing up a newspaper data center, worth invading her apartment. Worth killing her over.

Mark Dawson. A younger, grinning Mark Dawson.

Her body tensed, wanting to investigate the lead immediately. But then Nate would come with her. His knee was already bothering him after their sprint. He'd already been shot at, endangered, because of her story. Because of her.

She wanted to comfort him the only way she knew how, the only way that would work. Her lips found his shoulder, his chest. Her hands worked over the ridge of his abs, lower.

"I want you too much," he said hoarsely, his voice a rough caress in the dark. "I couldn't be gentle with you. I couldn't…stop."

He didn't need to move for what she had planned. She pulled the sheet down, moving between his legs. She heard his breath catch, felt the hitch in his body. "Let me," she whispered.

He groaned. "Fuck, gorgeous. You ruin me."

His words ricocheted through her body. She was ruining him—and she'd have to leave him. That was the only way to keep him safe.

Not tonight, though. Tonight he was hers.

She put her fists around his cock, already thick and throbbing beneath her touch. He rocked into her hands, thrusting upward. She slowed her strokes, bending down to kiss the tip of his cock.

A low growling sound rent the air. "Suck me, gorgeous. Take me in that sweet mouth. I need you."

Still she teased him, letting her tongue lap the satiny crown, resisting.

Then his hands tangled in her hair. With a grunt he pulled her down. She opened her mouth as he slid inside, leaving the salty proof of his arousal on her tongue. Powerful hips thrust up in small increments, his control strained, thigh muscles trembling beneath her palms.

He found the rhythm he wanted, and in those

melodic moments she found the surrender she needed. It was a joining, a fight, pulling her close even while he stole her breath. Every moment they had spent apart tugged her scalp, his hands in her hair. And every sweet moan and helpless grunt drew her back to him.

She only had time to register the slide of his crown as he left, the absence of him, before he flipped her over on the bed. She turned quickly, landed softly, the front of her body cradled in sheets warm from him. His hands spanned her hips, fingertips bruising; then her hips were in the air.

He shoved a pillow under her, his movements jerky.

Her hands opened and closed against the sheets, grasping nothing. "Nate?"

"Let me," he said roughly, mirroring her request.

How could she deny him? She could refuse him nothing, not even when he mounted her from behind, his cock a thick presence at her entrance.

His thrust forced a sharp sound from her throat, both protest and retreat. "Too much," she gasped out. "Wait."

He pulled back out and pushed in harder,

faster. "Can't," he grunted. "Can't stop."

She squeezed her eyes together, forcing hot tears onto the bed. It wasn't the worst pain she'd ever felt, wasn't close to the foreign burn of strange men, the flash of red bandannas. But God, somehow it hurt the most. As if she could feel every sting of betrayal, of violence, that was buried deep inside the man behind her. He pushed his own darkness into her, and she took it, she took it—she reveled in the jagged edges of it.

His fingers dug into her hips, pulling her back as he thrust forward. She couldn't have controlled this any more than she could have made the ocean stay still. He moved her as soundly, as surely as nature itself, and she floated on the force of him.

She didn't know how long she drifted that way, her body impaled on his, around him, holding whatever shape he gave her. All she saw was darkness, all she heard was the slap of flesh. All she felt was *him,* his weight and presence surrounding her, his need lapping at her skin.

Her orgasm swept over her in a rush of arousal. The word *climax* lost meaning. There was no shape to her, no beginning and, God, no end. Her inner muscles vibrated in helpless response. She came for minutes, for hours, the whole damn night while he fucked her from behind like a machine.

No, not like a machine. A machine would be mindless, unfeeling. He came apart behind her, holding on to her like she was the only thing that could put him back together. His emotions filled the shadows of the room, enemies lurking in every innocent corner, danger an intimate companion.

When at least he came, he roared with both pain and pleasure, with a haunting release that reverberated through her, a rare and precious peek into the heart of a man. Not just any man. *This man.* This soldier. This fighter. This jaded hero who wanted to stop caring, but he just couldn't. A lesser man would have turned away from the world, would have crumpled under the weight of his injuries, his loss. But Nate cared about his country, the people in it, so deeply. He couldn't stop, just like she couldn't stop loving him. Breaking up hadn't changed that. Nothing would.

But how could she be with him, when it put him in danger? She needed to go after Mark Dawson, needed to nail Moreland now more than ever. How could she risk Nate's life?

Her brother had died for her.

She wouldn't let Nate die too.

CHAPTER TWENTY

HE WOKE HER in the night, his lips on the back of her neck, his body hard and wanting behind her. His large hand slipped down her stomach before he touched between her legs. She was already wet for him, already soft with desire. Her hips rocked into his hand, begging for more pressure. Coarse fingertips circled her clit until she sobbed her release.

He started to climb over her, but she stopped him. "Wait."

His eyes on her were hot as she left the bed, naked, and crossed to the black bag of weaponry and equipment. She bypassed the guns and ammo and knives. She'd been looking for handcuffs, but rope would have to do.

When she stalked back to the bed with the twine of black rope in her hands, he gave her a devastating grin. "You want me to tie you up?"

God, yes, please. Her body turned liquid at the thought of being at his mercy. Except she needed something else more than pleasure. She needed redemption.

"Something like that," she said, straddling his large body.

Maybe he didn't worry because he was so much stronger than her. Or maybe it was just a testament to how much he trusted her, but he didn't stop her from tying his wrists to the bed frame. Instead his lips captured her nipple, sending sparks of desire to her core.

It was a knot he had taught her, the couple of times they'd gone out on Lake Travis.

Then she leaned back, examining his muscled body, all tied up. She would have wanted him to tie her up, but she couldn't deny the beauty this way. His arms were a work of art, his chest broad and strong, his waist tapered with tight muscle.

"Fuck, you're gorgeous this way," he muttered, studying her body.

A blush heated her cheeks, probably all the way down to her breasts. Her nipples tightened under his heated gaze. "You know I care about you."

He stilled beneath her. "God, Sofia."

She hesitated, feeling torn. "I think I love you."

A grunt, a recoil, as if she'd punched him in

the stomach. "You're telling me this now, when I'm tied up."

Without answering, she bent and pressed her lips to the center of his chest, then down his abs, until she reached his cock. A single kiss to the tip, licking the salty pearl away. An apology. A goodbye.

"I'm sorry," she said.

"Fuck, fuck. Don't be sorry, gorgeous." His eyes darkened, arms straining against the bonds. But she'd tied them tight, using knots he had shown her. He wouldn't get free. "I love you too. I've been going fucking crazy wanting you. Always half a second away from going to your house and begging you to take me back—or fuck, from tying you to the bed."

That made her smile. "It would have been good that way. Better than this."

Then she backed up off the bed.

Awareness seeped into his hot gaze. "What are you doing?"

"I have to go, and I can't...I can't let you get hurt."

"Jesus, Sofia. You think if you take one wild risk after another that you'll stop being that girl in the closet, that victim? Do you? That if you take down enough fuckers like Moreland, you'll finally win?"

She blinked, somehow not surprised that he had her figured out. She'd whispered her darkest fears to him under cover of night, naked in every sense of the word. It didn't change anything. "I'm sorry."

Nate's eyes burned. "Because you'll always be that girl, Sofia. But the thing is, I love that girl. She fucking survived. She's beautiful and strong. And I need her to stay alive, so *stay with me.*"

It always came back to that, the way he had wanted her to choose between him and the paper, the way he'd wanted her to back down from a fight. Except how could she truly be strong if she was always afraid? "I'm sorry," she repeated softly, meaning it this time.

He must have seen the determination in her eyes, because he fought the rope with a curse. "Don't do this, Sofia. Don't fucking do this to me."

She turned and got dressed, ignoring his cursing and the ominous clanging of the bed frame against the cheap wall. But she knew this was the best for him. That made it easier for her to slip out of the room, locking the door behind her.

✧   ✧   ✧

THEN IT WAS just a matter of walking to the closest bus stop.

She felt a little bad about taking his cell phone, but he'd thrown away the SIM card in hers. He would be able to track his phone eventually, but she hoped she'd be done before then.

The first call she made was to Remy. Voice mail.

"Remy, it's me. Where are you? Shit's getting crazy."

Moreland is dirty, and I think I figured out the link he doesn't want us to find. It has something to do with Dawson Tech, and I'm heading over there now. That was what she wanted to say, but she couldn't be sure they weren't listening. She couldn't risk endangering her friend before she knew Remy was safe.

"Be careful," she said before hanging up.

Then she called Andre, who picked up on the second ring. "Who is this?"

"Sofia Mendes."

"Fuck," he said. "Where the hell are you?"

"I'm on the move," she said, not sure how much to give away.

"Well, get in here," he barked. "They found men at your apartment. One dead. One in custody."

"I can't come in yet. There's something I have to check out."

"Fuck, Sofia. I already thought you were dead once. Come straight here. We can get you protection."

Not against this. "I'll call you when I know more."

He swore again. "Is Remy with you?"

Her blood went cold. "No. Was she injured in the blast?"

"That was me, laid up in the hospital. She came to visit me; I remember that much." A heavy pause. "And then she fucking disappeared."

I wouldn't want her to end up as one of my...investments.

Was that what had happened to Remy? She hadn't been on the Moreland story, but she had sat across from Sofia. Maybe it was open season on anyone who even knew her. Or maybe Remy had actually found a clue, something that connected Moreland to the explosion.

The bus pulled up to the curb, its interior gleaming dully against the night.

"I have to go," she said, interrupting his protests. "I'll be careful."

On the bus she used the phone's browser to

look up the article she had written for the *Daily*. There was a quote from Mark Dawson. *I do whatever I can to help women advance in technology, within limits. My first priority is to my company, of course.*

Christ, he even talked like Moreland.

How had she not seen it before? Unfortunately, there was no shortage of men who used bullshit doublespeak. And then the tech article had been a few years ago. She'd seen no connection on the surface between a rich tech CEO who drove a Tesla and a senator who had dirty ties to Mexico. Clearly there was something deep, something dark, between them.

The bus took her toward the outer edges of downtown, the stop abandoned and dark. There weren't even streetlights leading into the night. A cab could have brought her closer, but she couldn't risk being seen.

Birds hooted from shadowed trees. Small shuffles in the gravelly terrain told her rodents were awake. Judging by the size of one possum, its eyes bright, some of those rodents were as big as dogs. She shivered, walking faster.

Would Nate have gotten free? She'd only been gone thirty minutes, at most.

He'd be furious with her, but he'd be safe.

Her footsteps sounded loud by the time the glass building pierced the horizon, its glass windows glinting in moonlight. *Crunch, crunch, crunch.* She moved farther away from the road, where coarse brush at least hid her steps more than the rocky ground.

As she rounded a hill, the parking lot came into view. Empty, of course.

Not many workers in the office in the middle of the night.

So what did she expect to find? She didn't know. She *couldn't* know. This was what Andre had taught her, to follow the clues no matter where they took her. And it was what Nate had taught her, to give them two sentences and then write whatever the fuck she wanted.

This was *her* story.

Whatever was happening, it was coming to a head. With Moreland in town, with his *inventory* at risk, this was her best chance to find out the truth.

And if she didn't find out, she would forever be in limbo, the threat looming over her head. She would have failed her mission as a journalist.

In some way, she felt that she would fail Nate too. He'd fought for freedom on foreign soil. This was her part, fighting crime and corruption right here in America. Maybe if she actually did this, she would be equal to him. Maybe she would be *worthy* of him.

Worthy even after what had happened to her.

She circled the building, expecting to search through trash bins to find anything. But then, this was her work. It wasn't always glamorous, but at least no one shot at her.

Voices drifted to her over the sound of her own breath.

She froze. Part of her wanted it to be a trick of the wind. Another part of her knew that this was where something would happen. This was the link he was hiding. Now she would find out why.

Quietly, quietly, she crept closer, still tucked behind dense foliage that surrounded the building, part of the design's tribute to nature that *would* have been the focal point of her article on the groundbreaking, if she hadn't changed it.

More voices. Her stomach formed a tight knot.

The person speaking wasn't Mark Dawson.

It wasn't even Stephen Moreland.

Oh God, it almost sounded like…Remy. Her friend. Her fellow reporter. How was this possible? Horror crept into her veins, and the gentle hillside breeze felt like zero degrees.

"I told you to take care of him," said a male voice. Moreland?

"And I did," Remy said. "He's not going to talk until the shipment is gone."

"If you'd done what you were supposed to, he wouldn't talk ever again."

Who were they talking about? Dawson? They spoke faster and harder, as if in anger. An argument? Damn it, she needed to know. Sofia crept closer, heart beating so loud she could barely hear anything.

"She's still out there," came another male voice.

"Don't worry about her." Remy.

"I'm not worried," Moreland said. "This is the end of the line. No more shipments. No more bullshit. No more nosy little reporters who don't know when to quit."

"And the last job," Remy said.

"Of course." That sounded like it was said with a smile.

Sofia's chest constricted with pain, with betrayal. There had been fear that Remy had been hurt. And there'd been a sliver of hope that she'd actually uncovered some clue, on the trail as one of the best reporters Sofia knew. But the fear and the hope had turned into anger.

Remy was working for them.

She needed to call Nate. She should call Andre.

She had to—

A click from behind her. Something hard pressed against her head. "End of the line," came a voice she distantly recognized as Mark Dawson. "Guess you really don't know when to quit."

CHAPTER TWENTY-ONE

SOFIA HAD A lot more sympathy for Nate as she twisted her hands. Her wrists ached from pulling them against the tight ropes, her skin on fire, rubbed raw. They had left her in some kind of large shed with equipment that was hard to make out in the dark. Maybe riding lawn mowers. Which meant there might be clipping shears somewhere in here, but she couldn't move an inch. Her hands were tied behind her, so tight she already felt pins in her shoulders as they went numb. More black rope tied her ankles to the chair legs.

Remy hadn't been able to meet her eyes.

How long had she been here? An hour. Maybe two.

Oh Nate, I'm sorry. Sofia wasn't sorry that she'd left him tied up. She had no doubt that if he'd come with her, he would be tied up too. Or maybe they'd just have shot him on sight. There had been more men with Dawson, hired guns like the ones who had invaded her apartment.

No, she was sorry that she'd ever walked away from him.

It had only been a few months apart, but they could have spent that time together. It would have been worth it, even knowing there'd be heartache at the end. He hadn't liked her job, but she would have stood her ground. She would have, if she hadn't been so determined to prove something to herself, to the world, after what had happened to her. Not just another broken girl. Not a victim. And now she was tied up in a warehouse, so she'd lost that fight.

And she'd lost Nate.

A scratch came from behind her. Oh God, that was all she needed, some kind of possum or rat who wanted to nibble at her feet. It could be something worse, something bigger. Like a coyote. The Hill Country was still largely wooded out here, with deer crossings commonplace. And where there were deer...

That was kind of the point of the ultra-natural landscaping. How ironic that she'd ended up in a place to care for those native shrubs, the ones she was supposed to write about.

The sound came again, louder this time. More of a long drag against the cement floor. It seemed to drag along her spine. Her heart pounded, beating up into her throat, almost pulsing in her eyelids. She'd already been held at gunpoint, threatened, tied up—nothing else should make her afraid, but she still felt like a teenaged girl hiding in the closet.

Her gaze darted over the bulky shadows until a slender silhouette formed.

"Remy," she gasped, part in relief, part in anger.

"I'm so sorry," Remy whispered. "I never wanted you to be hurt."

Maybe she'd wanted Remy to deny her involvement, despite what she'd heard before, because Sofia's gut clenched in disappointment. "How could you?"

Something glinted in the dark—a knife?

Remy knelt in front of her and tugged at the rope around her ankles. "I told you not to go after Moreland."

"And you knew that I couldn't stop."

The other ankle now. "Well, you have to now. They won't tie you up next time."

Sofia waited while Remy circled to cut her hands free. Then she stood and backed up. "You have to know I won't. How did you get involved with them, Remy? Is this about money?"

Remy made a dismayed sound, maybe insulted. "It's a long story."

"I've got time." Especially since Moreland had taken her phone.

A sigh, and Remy's shadow sat down on a box of undetermined contents. "My sister."

The image of Diego's face flashed through Sofia's mind, that red bandanna he wore until the very end. "I didn't know you had a sister."

"Allison was older than me. We were close when we were little. Then she got older, got messed up with a fucked-up crowd. Drugs. Sex. That kind of thing."

A sick feeling settled into her stomach. This sounded too close to Sofia's story, a parallel. She sat down beside Remy. "What happened?"

"Spring break. Cancun. And she never came back."

"Oh my God."

"My parents pretended that she'd run away, maybe met a boy and lived a life of sin and alcohol. That way they could judge her, while still believing she had chosen that. But I knew something worse had happened to her."

"That's horrible, Remy. I'm so sorry."

Remy shook her head. "You don't understand. I told her to go. She had wanted us to spend time together that week. But I'd been pissed at her for spending so much time with her friends lately. I told her that if she loved her friends so much, she should go with them."

And so Remy blamed herself for what had happened to her sister.

"It wasn't your fault," Sofia said softly.

"I told her I didn't care about her!"

Sofia looked down, swallowing hard. She had always felt guilty for the way her brother had died, even though he'd done it to protect her. And he'd felt guilty for what his gang brothers had done to her, even though it wasn't really his fault. They were all just adrift, at the mercy of the dark forces around them.

Except that Remy was helping them.

"Moreland is mixed up with human trafficking," Sofia said, putting the pieces together.

"I started tracking her down as soon as I got into college. Spent every break in Mexico, learning the language, making contacts." A rough laugh. "Part of me wanted them to take me too, because then at least I'd know what happened to her."

Sofia knew how the guilt could make you reckless, how you could almost want the pain, believe you deserve it. Maybe that was how she'd ended up in this warehouse, after all.

"Then I tracked it to Moreland," Remy said. "I was already graduated by then, working at the *Daily*. I begged Andre to give me the story, but he thought it would seem like favoritism."

Sofia gasped softly. "Because you were together."

Remy looked away. "Together. I guess you could say that. Not that it helped me in the end. Not that it helped him either. He was hurt in the blast, did you know that?"

"Shit."

"Yeah. And it's my fault, because I should have nailed Moreland when I had the chance. Should have shot him in the fucking heart."

"Why didn't you?" Sofia had always wanted to play by the rules, had believed in them like Nate had once believed in them—with an idealism that was destined to break. But Remy had always had a dark streak in her eyes, a determination that Sofia knew to take seriously.

"He has my sister," Remy said softly. "He has Allison."

Her throat tightened. "Are you sure?"

"There were…pictures." A rough sound. "He said if I did things for him, I could get her back. I thought I could do it, that I could keep everyone safe and save her too. That I could still nail him when it was over."

Sofia ached with the knowledge that her friend had been up against so much, facing it alone. There was anger still, a sense of betrayal. But she knew that she'd have done the same to save the people she loved.

"Where are they now?"

"I don't know," Remy said, her voice dull. "They think I'm on my way to the *Daily* to spin some bullshit story about Moreland's wonderful speech. Every time he says this is the last job, but it never ends."

"He'll never give her back," Sofia said softly, gently, but her friend had to know. Allison would be the smoking gun that would put Moreland away forever.

"I know that, but there's a shipment coming through tonight. I don't know where it is, but if I can find it, if I can get the girls away from him, that might be the leverage I need to get her back."

And to expose him as a monster. "Do you have a car?"

"Why?"

"I have a few places we can check. Some warehouses owned by the same shell corporation that owns that mansion in Austin."

Remy gasped. "You didn't tell me there were warehouses too."

"I didn't realize we were working on the same story," Sofia said in a dry voice. "I checked them out, but they were empty. I bet they aren't empty now."

Chapter Twenty-Two

NATE CRACKED THE last piece of wood on the metal door. The bedpost split in half, splintering across the thin carpet. That gave him enough slack to wrench one hand from the loop. He'd managed to split the cheap frame in two before using the door as a reverse hammer.

The rope fell onto the floor.

Fuck, he had taught her that knot.

He grabbed the hotel phone and made a call to Josh's secure line. "She's gone."

"What do you mean, gone?" his friend asked. "They took her."

Nate grimaced. "She left. Tied me to the bed. Took off with my phone. I need you to track it. And send a motherfucking car for me."

Only the sound of quiet laughter answered him. "Tied you…to the bed…"

He waited, furious that he'd let her get away. Or maybe he was more furious that she had sprung the L-word when she'd been about to leave him. Again. "She could be in danger," he ground out. "So if you could pull your head out of your ass, maybe?"

"Sorry," Josh said, not sounding sorry. "I'll send a car for you. And clothes?"

"I have clothes," Nate growled out before hanging up the phone.

Then he packed his gear and headed out the door. Someone from the next room peeked out their blinds. Clearly they'd heard him rip apart the bed frame like the fucking Hulk.

He stalked the nearest bus route until he found the driver who'd picked her up, though he couldn't remember her stop. It had taken him long enough that her trail was cold.

Hopefully Josh came through with the fucking trace.

Josh didn't just send a car. He came himself, pulling up alongside where Nate had started walking toward campus. The tinted window rolled down, revealing the grinning bastard. "I think I'm in love," the bastard said.

Nate opened the door and slung his body inside. "She's taken."

He might be pissed at her, but that didn't mean he was giving her up.

Even if his friend was fucking kidding. But he

couldn't be sure, because anyone with half a brain could see how amazing Sofia was. He could still feel her body above him, breasts hanging with dark nipples, hair spilling around her shoulders. Her eyes had been a fucking siren's, calling to him. He'd almost come just looking at her. And when she'd left him there, her determination like goddamn armor around her slender body, he hadn't been any less turned on.

Josh handed over a new phone. "They turned your phone off, probably thinking we can't track it that way. But since it's yours, it's got a separate signal."

"So where the fuck is she?" He was having a hard time ignoring the black panic, imagining Sofia in danger, in enemy hands. Hurt, abused. The way she had been before.

"Some warehouses on the east side. My intel doesn't show anything, but we'll go directly there. I have two other teams en route, but they're farther away than us."

At least Josh knew how to run a fucking op. "I'm going in."

He couldn't risk waiting for the woman he loved. *I think I love you.*

He was going to make her pay for that in the most delicious, depraved ways he could think up.

Josh gave him a sideways glance. "You're too close to this."

"I'm going in," he ground out.

At least Josh stopped arguing, communicating with his teams via radio. He'd pulled them back from other cities when he realized shit was going down tonight, but they were still an hour out. Too long.

"Fine," Josh finally said. "We'll go in together."

"No." He couldn't risk his friend getting killed, especially without backup. He knew the risks when he went in, but that didn't mean Josh had to take them. "You wait for your team."

Josh snorted. "You can't have it both ways. Either we both wait or we go in together."

This was the part Nate hated most about black ops. At least with his cover, the PI gig, he got to work alone. Relying on his teammates, having them rely on him, took him back to that fucking hut every time.

He imagined her tortured body. All that gorgeous tan skin he'd seen just hours ago—broken, violated. They couldn't wait, not for any reason. If it took him back to the hut, so fucking what.

They parked two miles away and armed themselves to the teeth.

Anyone who got between him and Sofia was going down. Anyone who laid a finger on her? Down. Simple as that. Josh communicated their plans to the rest of the teams before going dark, so they could go in silent.

The warehouses were long abandoned, signs faded and fallen, the alleys strewn with old debris. That was the point, for someone as dirty as Moreland.

Seclusion. Secrecy. This was how he operated.

The first guard Nate came across didn't see him coming. Nate had him in a headlock, knocked out, then gagged and tied, before he could let out a shout.

Josh gave a curt nod and left to repeat the procedure as many times as necessary.

A window clouded with grit gave them a clear view of exactly why Moreland needed that secrecy. Women, just like Sofia had said. Nate had always known she was a fucking amazing reporter, but the fact that she'd blown open such a dark operation was a new level. And it might have gotten her killed.

He scanned the bodies huddled along a wall, most naked, some with dirty rags.

She wasn't there.

"No visual," he murmured, barely a breath, as

Josh joined him from his perimeter check.

"Four down," Josh murmured back, meaning he'd taken out four guards patrolling the outside.

"I'm counting five more inside. Plus a guy I don't recognize."

Josh took in the girls against the wall with a curse. "Looks like, what? Thirty of them? Jesus fuck."

It complicated things because they couldn't allow them to be hurt. Sofia was the most important things in Nate's mind, but he knew the captive women had just become the priority. Without a visual on Sofia, they had to act on what they could see.

He sent up a small prayer to the God he had long ago turned away from that she would be safe in the meantime. "Should we wait for your teams?"

Josh ran a hand over his face, clearly shaken by the sight of those women tied up. "We don't know what could happen in the meantime. What they've already been through."

Extracting one woman would have been risky enough, but thirty? "They'll be safer with backup."

Josh studied them, his expression grim in the dim glow of the grimy window. "You'd have gone in for Sofia. We don't know these women, but they don't deserve anything less. We go in."

Nate nodded, knowing he would back up his friend regardless of his decision. The same way that Josh had been willing to back him up. There were some benefits to having a team.

In a matter of minutes, they worked through a takeover strategy. Nate would enter through the front, taking down two of the men and drawing fire away from the women. He'd have the element of surprise, but he'd be vulnerable that way.

Josh would use the back entrance, taking down the remaining guards with stealth. Then he'd usher the women out of the building and attempt to secure them near the SUV until backup arrived.

"Ready," Nate said, his mind focused on his task.

He couldn't think about Sofia, couldn't worry what was happening to her.

Josh deliberated for one second. Then he nodded. "Five seconds."

He disappeared around the corner, and Nate took his position near the front entrance.

In ops like this, making the plan took longer than actually executing it. Everything happened in a matter of seconds, the entire action over in minutes. His brain reverted to the old flip-book style of processing, slowing down everything to snapshots.

Five. Four. Three. Two. One.

The burst of light when he opened the door.

Splatter of red as one guard went down.

Whizz of bullets as he took aim. The second guard went down.

Out of the corner of his eye, he saw Josh take down the last two guards. Exactly as they'd planned. Everything executed with precision, just as he'd been trained, just as he'd known they were capable of. Except for the unknown, the unexpected whine of an aircraft when his team was there to rescue him. The blast.

No unexpected sounds came, no blast.

"This way," Josh said, taking charge of the women.

They huddled away from him until Nate pulled off his mask. "We're here to help."

Whatever they saw in Nate's eyes, they must have decided to trust them. They ran out the door, following Josh while Nate took up the rear.

The last girl huddled in the corner, clearly not won over.

His blood whipped through his veins, some latent sense telling him they were running out of time. He crouched near her and put his hand out. "I'm not going to hurt you, I swear."

She shook her head, wrapping dirty arms around herself.

Fuck.

The sound came to him as the whimpers and padding footsteps of the other girls died away. The whir of a vehicle stopping near the front door. He could only pray that Josh had gotten the other girls far enough, because backup had arrived. He had a sneaking suspicion that it wasn't Josh's backup, but more of Moreland's men. They must have been dispatched when the men bleeding out on the ground stopped responding.

"We have to go," he said urgently.

The girl curled in on herself, lost to him. He realized that he'd have to pick her up, physically remove her. He hated to touch her against her will, but it was life or death. She fought him, scratching, screaming, and he knew that whatever stealth he might have had was gone. He hefted her into an awkward carry, while she struggled to get free.

He was halfway to the exit when he felt something sharp blast his shoulder.

Stumbling, he dropped her. "Run," he managed to gasp.

At least she obeyed that much. The last thing he saw was the flash of her hair through the door.

Pain seared him—*fuck, he was hit.*

Nate forced himself to turn over and shoot toward the front, blind and desperate to give them a few more seconds to safety. Two men surrounded him. Maybe he could have taken them, maybe not. With his shoulder on fire, he didn't have a shot.

The first kick to his stomach took his breath away.

The one to his back hit his kidney, and he saw black spots.

He managed to swipe the guy in front of him with his leg. The next boot met his face with an audible crack, and he knew he was going to die here. His only hope was Josh's backup teams, but by his internal clock they still had another fifteen minutes. His knee hadn't been recently shattered this time, he hadn't been starved, but he had fought enough to recognize defeat.

In that godforsaken hut, he'd accepted death.

Even welcomed it.

Sofia's gorgeous face flashed in front of his eyes, and he knew he wouldn't accept this. Fuck no, he wouldn't die. Not while he wasn't sure she was safe. Not while she was in this world. He would fight for every single fucking second with her.

His entire body screamed in pain as he pushed up on his hands. The guy went for the easy kick—right to his stomach. Nate was prepared for it, gripping the leg and twisting hard. The man screamed, but underneath Nate heard the snap of bone breaking.

The other guy was on top of him in a matter of seconds.

The smart thing would have been to whip out his gun and shoot him, but these guys assumed that because he was wounded, he'd be an easy kill. They were the kind of fuckers in the hut, the ones who enjoyed inflicting pain. Nate would show them that he wasn't easy.

He whipped his elbow into one guy's eye socket, eliciting a hard grunt.

Then he got a knee in the groin and gasped his own pain.

The sound of a car pulling up whispered through the warehouse. More reinforcements for these fuckers? Except they tensed, as if they weren't expecting company. And Josh's teams would still be ten minutes away. So who had come? Who was unaccounted for?

The assholes on top of him were clearly just as

curious. They backed away, ducking behind some empty crates like fucking cockroaches.

Nate blinked through the sweat and the blood, struggling to focus on the open door.

And then he saw her, like some kind of fucking mirage. The object of his dreams, the woman he loved. Sofia. He wanted her to be fake, because God, fuck, she couldn't be here.

Her gaze met his, and he knew she was real.

Horror filled those gorgeous dark eyes. "Oh my God, Nate."

"No, Sofia. No!"

He was too late. It was happening again. He saw it happening in sharp, vivid increments—the men behind the crates finally pulling out their fucking guns. Sofia's attention on Nate's body, his injuries, his *weakness*.

This was like before, when he'd been unable to warn his team, when they'd gotten caught in the cross fire while trying to rescue him. Sofia was here, rushing to his side, about to be hurt because he couldn't protect her.

Worse than death, seeing Sofia hurt.

He couldn't, wouldn't let it happen.

From somewhere deep, he found enough strength to drag his broken body upright. His knee may as well have been hit with another fucking hammer, because it felt shattered. His body was in pieces, but his heart was finally whole.

He launched himself on top of Sofia. Surprised, she went down under him. He was her shield, the only form of protection he had left to offer. There were loud bangs, gunfire, and he prayed he would be enough.

Chapter Twenty-Three

SOFIA PUSHED AT the heavy weight, but Nate was pure muscle. It took all her strength, all her effort, just to move him sideways. Then her hands were running over him—his beautiful face, already bruised, broken, his arms, his chest. Searching for a bullet hole, because she'd heard those shots. She found it in his shoulder, an entry through the back, no exit.

"Oh God," she whispered, tears clouding her vision. "Nate, Nate, Nate."

He groaned. "Fuck, Sofia."

Men in black shirts and cargo pants had invaded the warehouse suddenly, milling around her. They surrounded the two men who'd jumped out from behind the crates. The ones Nate had protected her from.

Josh approached, his expression grave. "How is he?"

"Strong enough to kick your ass, asshole," Nate said, his words slurring together.

"Don't you dare die on me, Nate. I'm serious."

His grin was lopsided, as if he were drunk. "You're gorgeous."

"He's punch-drunk," Josh said, sounding amused. "Probably a concussion. We need to get that bullet wound checked out though."

Instead, Nate pushed himself to sit. He glanced over at the men who were being disarmed, their hands behind their heads, facing the ground. He made a growling sound. "I ought to feed those fuckers their own dicks. They tried to hurt you."

"You can't kill them," she told him. "We need their help to find the women."

Josh gave her a small smile. "We've already got them."

Only then did she realize Remy wasn't with her. "Remy…"

"Your friend?" Josh nodded toward the back exit. "Think she was looking for someone. My men have them covered. They're safe. And an ambulance is on the way."

Relief swept through her, and she turned to Nate. "Don't move."

"So bossy," he murmured.

She ran her fingertips over his lips. "Hush

now."

"Not gonna let you tie me up again."

The laugh that came out of her was part happiness, part worry. She needed him to be okay. *I think I love you.* That was what she'd told him in the motel. Bending her head, she whispered in his ear, "You're my hero, Nate."

His hazy eyes focused on her. "That's right, gorgeous. Not gonna let you go, either."

His lids closed, and she gasped. "Nate. Nate!"

Josh knelt beside her, pressing two fingers to Nate's neck. "Passed out. This fucker survived the worst. He's not going to let this get him."

She heard the anxiety beneath the steel and realized Josh was nervous, though he tried to hide it. That made her nervous, but also glad that Nate had friends—coworkers, technically—who cared about him that much. Dipping her head, she pressed her forehead to his cheek. "Hold on, Nate. Just a little longer."

Time passed in shuddering stops and starts, her breath attuned to his.

She didn't know how long she knelt like that, but eventually Josh placed a hand on her back. Paramedics had a stretcher beside her, ready to pull Nate away. She stumbled moving out of their way, her legs numb.

She held his hand on the way to the ambulance, keeping him warm, keeping him company as best she could. He was still unconscious when they wheeled him into surgery, taking him away from her.

Her head rested in her hands, her dark hair creating a curtain.

The scent of stale coffee drifted close, and she looked up. Remy was standing there, holding out a small Styrofoam cup with gray liquid.

Sofia lifted an eyebrow. "Is that coffee?"

"I know it tastes like shit, but it's better than nothing."

Conceding the point, Sofia took the cup with quiet thanks. One sip, a grimace. Another sip. It was better than nothing. She needed something to stay alert, because Nate might be in surgery for hours.

The coffee settled into the right parts of her brain. "Did you find her? Your sister?'

Remy's face fell. "No. I showed her picture to the girls, but they hadn't seen her."

She set the coffee down and stood to—what? Hug her? They didn't have that kind of friendship, and Remy stepped back.

"I'm sorry," Sofia murmured.

Remy looked away. "I knew it was a long

shot. Anyway, I just came to say goodbye. I might be going away for a while."

Only then did the uniformed officers register. They hovered at the entrance to the waiting room, watching Remy like they expected her to make an escape attempt with old magazines and a watercolor painting.

Sofia blinked. "They can't lock you up. You were doing those things under duress. He blackmailed you. Moreland is the culprit here."

"Oh, they have him in custody. He lawyered up fast, but the evidence is mounting. It will be a while before they sort it out. I'm not going to withhold what I know and leverage a deal, though. I figure the more I cooperate, the better chance they have of actually finding her."

Sofia took a moment to consider that. "You're a hero, you know. I don't care what they say. You did what you thought was right."

Remy looked down before meeting her eyes. "Your intern might not agree with that."

"What?"

"I'm sure he'll tell you about it. Maybe even get a byline out of it. That's not the point. The point is that you're the hero. I knew if I gave you the link to Dawson, you'd dig until you found the truth. And that's what happened."

So Remy had been the one to encrypt those hidden photos. Sofia may have found out the truth, but only with help—from Remy, from Nate. *God, Nate. Stay strong for me.*

Remy turned to leave but paused. "Just do one thing for me. I let my past fuck up my future. Don't make the same mistake, okay? Not with Nate."

"I won't," Sofia whispered, but she didn't know if she'd get the chance to make things right. He might hate her after she'd left him at the motel, he might blame her for getting him shot.

He might never wake up.

Chapter Twenty-Four

THE WORLD SWAM in blacks and blues, a mix of pain and grief. He wasn't sure what was real and what was dream—his team around him, broken flesh. Sofia's gorgeous body, bruised and battered. He fought the heavy tide, but it only pushed him deeper.

"Nate? I'm here."

He knew that voice. *Sofia.* He wanted to talk to her, to tell her that he loved her. Again and again, he wanted to whisper his love, his praise, his fucking devotion. Except he couldn't open his eyes. A rough groaning sound met his ears, and he realized that was him.

"Are you hurting?" she whispered.

He felt something soft and warm on his hand, his arm. Her touch.

More, he demanded.

She responded with a kiss to his cheek.

Yes. Again.

This time she didn't answer, and it was

enough to make him struggle. He forced his eyes open, the light searing him. His eyelids weighed a fucking ton, but he was determined to see her. The world blurred in a miasma of beige and black. How drunk had he gotten?

Not drunk, he realized. Shot.

Sofia's face formed over him, those dark eyebrows and darker eyes, those gorgeous full lips he loved to claim. There were circles too, shadows of worry. How long had she been awake? Was she eating properly? Fuck, he wanted to take care of her.

"Sleep," he croaked.

"I know," she murmured, feathering her fingers over his brow. "You've been sleeping for days now. I'm so glad you're awake, baby."

That wasn't what he meant, but her hands felt amazing. "Don't stop."

The corner of her lips turned up. "The nurse is here."

He didn't want the nurse. "Want you."

She bent her head. "Dirty boy."

He grunted, yes.

"She needs to check on you now that you're awake. I'll be right here the whole time. I'm not leaving, okay?"

That was the last thing he heard before the

waters dragged him down again. He fought, but there were monsters there too, tentacles thick and strong, holding him underwater. *Don't leave, Sofia. I need you. I love you.*

When he woke again, the room was empty.

He studied the white walls and beeping machinery. Still in the hospital. And he felt like shit. Guess that was what getting shot and then kicked with boots did to a guy. Except where the fuck was Sofia?

The door opened, and he tensed with anticipation.

Josh strolled in, carrying a tray with two coffees and a white paper bag.

"Sofia," Nate demanded.

That just made him laugh. "Fuck you right back." He slung himself into the chair beside him, looking like some giant in a dollhouse. "Sorry, man, you're stuck with my ugly mug."

Nate grunted his disapproval.

Josh sent a glance down to Nate's shoulder, which was exposed, the white bandage fresh from this morning. "You got pretty fucked up."

He really wanted Sofia.

The bullet in his shoulder had fucked him up pretty good, like Josh said, but the kicks to his kidney had him spitting blood for the past week.

Only Sofia's gentle hands had kept him sane. So where was she?

Josh fiddled with the remote control and turned on the TV. He switched channels until Nate did a double take at the screen. Dressed in a sweater and skirt was the girl who had stolen his heart, the girl he wanted by his side. Sofia.

"Why didn't you wait for the cops?" the man in a suit asked.

They were sitting in upholstered chairs, a fake fireplace behind them. He vaguely recognized the set from a national news syndicate that Sofia used to watch.

Sofia learned forward, her dark eyes earnest. "We knew that Senator Moreland had public support. Any allegations would be met with red tape and lots of press. Meanwhile the traffickers who worked for him would have time to go underground. The most important thing was recovering those women while we had the chance."

Fuck, she was gorgeous.

Sofia had always maintained that she wouldn't be good as a TV reporter, that she was too shaky. And he had felt her shake in those moments in Josh's house after the shooting in her apartment.

She wasn't shaking now. Her hands were still,

her voice clear. The interviewer was looking at her with awe—and more than a little bit of desire. Nate narrowed his eyes at the fucker.

"She looks good," Josh commented, taking a sip of his coffee.

"Go to hell."

"She called me, you know. Worried that you'd wake up while she was gone. I think she hasn't left your bedside except to do the interview."

Damn. He couldn't stay laid up in this hospital bed, making her sleep in that uncomfortable metal chair. "Get me out of here."

"No can do, buddy. Sofia's orders."

He grunted. "You owe me."

Josh gave him a look. "You've been calling in a lot of favors lately. Lucky for you that you had racked up so many over the last ten years. I'll probably owe you until the day I die."

Damn right. "Where is she?"

Okay, so he turned a little caveman when he got injured.

Josh chuckled. "She's at the news station. You wanna surprise her? Because you can fucking surprise her."

Surprising her sounded good, because he hadn't forgotten the rope and the motel room. He needed to pay her back for that. More than that, he needed to tell her that he had let her push him away because he wasn't the man she needed. He hadn't been whole before, but he was now. It still made his heart freeze in fear to think of her in danger, but he'd be by her side as much as she would let him.

Chapter Twenty-Five

SOFIA HELD OUT her arms while the tech removed the microphone wire from her sweater. The interviewer's name was Brian James, an award-winning journalist who had pursued her story. She had finally relented, even if it meant leaving the hospital for a day trip, because she needed the truth out there. He conferred with people off the set, the illusion of a comfy sitting room stark against the hollow warehouse.

A series of articles she'd written would debut in the *Daily* starting on Sunday, thanks to Andre. But there was something to be said for the directness, the accessibility of the television.

Moreland had attempted to deny everything, but the evidence and public opinion turned against him. Pundits flooded the political talk shows denouncing him, declaring that they had always known something was wrong. Dawson had gotten further in his denials, claiming that he'd only been a contributor to Moreland's campaign.

Until a search warrant had uncovered a half-dozen women in the basement of his Austin mansion.

"Great interview," Brian said, removing his suit jacket.

"Thanks. That means a lot from you." He had a decade of experience on her, and she looked up to him.

He gave the tech a look, and he hurried away with her microphone. "Do you want to grab a drink? It helps me unwind after the tough stories."

Her eyebrows went up. Was he asking her on a date? "I'm sorry, but I need to get back to the hospital."

"Back to Nathaniel Gaines."

"Yes, back to Nate."

He nodded, a slight smile on his handsome face. "If that ever changes, be sure to look me up."

"Don't hold your breath," came a voice she recognized.

She whirled to see Nate standing there. A blink and he was still there. Not an illusion. She glanced back, but Brian was already walking away, a knowing glint in his eyes. He followed the sound guys out of the room, leaving them alone.

"What are you doing out of bed?" she demanded.

He glared at the door where Brian had just left. "That fucker."

She rolled her eyes. "You're going to pull your stitches out."

His gaze met hers, dark and intent. "I had to see you."

"I was going back in an hour!"

"An hour was too long." He glanced at the chair where she'd sat for the past hour and a half. "You were brilliant, by the way. Smart, passionate. Fucking gorgeous."

Heat flooded her cheeks. "You saw the interview?"

"You really thought Josh would keep me in the hospital?"

"I had hoped so, yeah."

That lopsided smile. He took a step forward, and she backed up. Another step and her legs were touching the interview chair. "What are you doing?" she asked.

He held up a loop of black rope. "Turnabout is fair play, gorgeous."

Her jaw dropped. "We're in a public place."

"I think what's his face got the message loud and clear. We won't be disturbed."

"His name is Brian James, and he's an award-winning national journalist, because this is a TV station!"

Nate glanced at the cameras, which had gone dark when Brian signed off. "You worried about a sex tape leaking out?"

For a minute she couldn't speak, shock and lust warring within her. "No," she managed. "I'm not worried about a sex tape, because we're not having sex. Not here."

He studied the plush chairs with a critical eye. "You're right. Too soft. You need something hard."

With that he took her hand and dragged her around the back wall of the set, into the dark cavern that the fake back created. Then his hand was on her jaw, cupping her, lifting her chin so that he could sip at her lips. His tongue teased the seam of her mouth until she went slack, letting him in, letting him back her up against the metal frame that formed the wall.

She melted against the cool ribbed metal, relishing the hard heat of him in front of her. Her body flamed with want, with need, the musky male scent of him triggering every feminine instinct.

His large hand drifted up her stomach, raising her sweater and exposing her bra. His thumb worked over the fabric, peaking her nipple. She gasped into his mouth, wanting more. Wanting exactly what he said: something hard. She needed him.

He pulled her wrist behind her back, and she froze. "Nate?"

His head lifted, revealing lust-drenched eyes. He pulled her other hand behind her back and worked the rope around her wrists. "Yes, gorgeous?"

"What are you doing?"

"Making something clear."

The knot tightened, holding her arms back. The position pushed her breasts forward into his chest. He looked at them with appreciation and pure carnal hunger. He ran one fingertip along the edge of her bra before tugging it down, exposing her pale flesh and tight nipple.

It was hard to swallow, even harder to form words. "Making what clear?"

He captured her nipple between his thumb and forefinger, rolling until her hips arched into him. His gaze remained direct on hers. "I let you go once. That was my mistake, but it's over now."

Her breath caught. "O-over?"

"Over. You're mine now. That means it's my responsibility. My right." He bent and licked her nipple, the slick texture of his tongue making her gasp. "My privilege to keep you safe."

Her moan was the only answer she could give.

"You want a fucking house in the hills?" he breathed against her neck. "You want a mansion? I have a pile of money sitting in the bank, because I never wanted anything. Only you."

His other hand pulled her skirt up, and then he groaned as his fingers felt bare skin. "Thigh highs. Fucking thigh highs. You know how hot it makes me when you wear these."

"I thought about you when I put them on," she whispered, but he'd been in a hospital bed. Too weak to do anything sexual yet, at least that was what she'd thought. Turned out he could dominate her with just a look.

Especially when he got on his knees. "Your knee," she said weakly.

He ignored her, pushing her skirt higher.

You think a busted knee is going to keep me from you? I could break every bone in my body and still fuck you just fine. I could be broken to shit, but I could still make you come with just my tongue.

He'd said that to her once, and he was proving it now. He'd been shot, beaten. He'd been to the brink of death, but he was here, making her body shudder and clench.

Blunt fingers pushed aside her panties, finding

her wet. "That's right," he murmured. "Give me something to drink."

A shiver ran through her. God, how she must look. Her breasts were exposed, her arms tied behind her back. The metal wall held her up, and then he bent his head. The first lick brought her to her toes. The second made her cry out.

"Louder," he muttered against her clit. "I want that fucker to hear you scream my name."

"Oh God," she sobbed, because it felt so good. She needed to be quiet, but he was licking her in the fast, insistent way that made her go crazy. Then his lips fastened around her clit, sucking her hard.

Her wordless sound echoed back to her.

"More," Nate demanded, sliding his finger inside her to the hilt. Her muscles clenched around him, holding him in, until he worked another finger inside. Then he stroked, finding that magic place, teasing her clit.

She rocked her hips against his face, moaning, begging. He'd been right when he said she needed something hard. He knew that about her. It had shamed her at first, but he had taught her to accept the pleasure where she found it—under his calloused hands, around his thick cock. At the edge of his teeth as they grazed her clit. The hint of danger brought her orgasm to the surface, and as pulses overtook her body, she screamed his name.

Chapter Twenty-Six

A SOUND JARRED Sofia from slumber. She didn't even remember falling asleep. The book she'd been reading lay askew on the pillow. The lamp cast an eerie glow against the dark window.

Another sound, this one clearer. The scuff of a shoe on hardwood?

It was barely there, maybe a whisper, but she felt something else. A presence. Her skin prickled with awareness that she was no longer alone.

Her phone was charging on the side table, but who would she call? She knew from experience that 911 wouldn't reach her in time if someone were truly inside her house. And Nate had to go dark during his missions, both for her safety and the safety of his team.

Her gaze darted to the closet, that deep part of her wanting to hide. To turn the flimsy lock as if that would be enough.

Except she was through being that girl.

She was stronger now—and infinitely more powerful. Nate had given her that. Thinking of him firmed her resolve.

In a smooth move, she rolled out of the bed and pulled the Sig from the side-table drawer. Her feet spread apart, her breath even. Only her heart betrayed any emotion, pounding through her veins like a war drum.

She took aim at the door as it eased open, casting a shadowed arc on the floor.

A man dressed in black stepped inside, combat boots on his feet, clearly armed based on his gait and the bulk at his sides. His broad shoulders and powerful chest tapered to a lean waist. The hard look in his eyes spoke to violence, to the capacity to kill.

Sofia dropped her arms and swore. "I could have shot you."

She had wanted to learn to shoot, but Nate had taken it one step further. He'd insisted that she be able to draw her gun in any situation at any time. And he liked to test her to drive his point home. Their training was dangerous and spontaneous and ridiculously sexy.

"Bulletproof vest," Nate said with a lopsided grin. In two strides he was in front of her, his hands cupping her face, his forehead pressed to hers. "Besides, you still had the safety on. We talked about that."

She tried to hold on to her anger—what if he'd been hurt? But all she felt was relief at the feel of him, the familiar musky scent of him. Relief and desire as her body fell under his thrall. "I missed you."

"Me too, gorgeous," he murmured.

She shoved the gun back into the drawer. "Well?"

"This is off the record, right?"

That earned him a raised eyebrow. "Do I have to tie you up again?"

A dangerous glint entered his eyes. "I'd love to see you try." With slow, careful movements, he took off his jacket, then his bulletproof vest. He hadn't been joking about that, at least. "But don't worry. I'll tell you about our *confidential* op."

Her eyes narrowed as she studied his stiff movements. "Oh God, you're hurt."

He gave her a scowl, which proved she was right. She helped him take off the thin black T-shirt and gasped at the bandages that circled his ribs. When he'd left two days ago the skin had still been yellow, almost tinged green, the aftermath of vicious bruises. Now it looked like he'd been injured even worse.

"It's only a fracture," he said.

"A rib fracture is a big deal!"

"Three ribs, technically."

The sound she made was a mixture of frustration and grief. "Oh, Nate."

He sat down, unable to fully hide his wince. Then he tugged her down beside him on the bed. "It was worth it. We found them."

Her heart seemed to expand. The lamp highlighted the scruff on his face, the exhaustion around his eyes, the pain in his body—all of which spoke to his heroism. Though it didn't make him comfortable to discuss, he no longer denied it either.

"Tell me," she said softly, her hand in his.

"There were more than they thought," he said grimly. "There were forty women in the hold. Two hostiles died in the exchange, four are sitting in FBI interrogation rooms right now. We also recovered the hard drives before they could wipe them."

Bittersweet hope tightened her throat. Those hard drives would mean they could find the women who were no longer being held by the human traffickers—the ones who had already been sold. "Thank you."

He glanced at her. "Allison was there."

Remy's sister. "Oh my God, that's amazing. She'll be so glad."

"She didn't want to see Remy. Refused, actually."

"Oh," Sofia said, swallowing past a lump in her throat. Remy had been reluctant to accept a deal. About as reluctant as the district attorney had been to prosecute a member of the press and the circus act that would have followed. In the end Remy's testimony had helped put away the big fish, and they'd settled on a plea for probation.

Remy still blamed herself for her sister's abduction.

And Andre still hadn't hired her back, leaving the desk empty months later.

"She doesn't blame Remy, does she?"

Nate shook his head, his eyes haunted. "I don't think so. The women…they've been through a lot. They're different now."

She rested her cheek against his shoulder, knowing that he understood that difference better than most. He'd been tortured, hurt. He had believed he would die in that jungle. And he would never be the same because of it. Not only his knee had been shattered in that horrible place.

But he had pieced himself back together,

made himself into someone stronger. Someone who had saved all those women. It wasn't only strength that won a fight. His bravery, his heart. That honor that refused to be knocked down.

"I know it must have been hard for you." To see those women, she meant.

His silence acknowledged that. Then, softly, "It will be hard for you too."

He knew where she'd be tomorrow and the days following, as the women were released from FBI custody. Some of the women would want to return to their families, to piece together some sense of normalcy.

Other women would want to tell their stories, and the world needed to hear them. For truth, for bravery. For every girl who had ever huddled in a closet.

"Tomorrow," she said softly.

Despite the amazing things Nate and his team had accomplished, there were more women to be rescued. More dragons to be slain. There was always another fight on the horizon. That knowledge didn't fill her with desperation like it had before, but with hope.

He nodded in agreement, turning her face to his. Every kiss he gave her was different, some hungry, some commanding. This one came with infinite tenderness, with never-ending promise.

"Tomorrow," he agreed.

"As long as you're with me, I can face anything."

It wasn't only the outside world that they had to fight. It was the fear they had inside, every time he left for a secret op, every time she pursued a story for the paper.

He brushed his thumb over her cheek, wiping away a tear she hadn't known she'd shed. "As long as you're with me, gorgeous, I have a reason to fight."

THE END

Thank you so much for reading Anti Hero! I hope you love Nate and Sofia's suspenseful story. Remember Nate's military brother in arms, Josh? You can read his book AUDITION now…

Blood and sweat. Bethany Lewis danced her way out of poverty. She's a world class athlete… with a debt to pay.

Joshua North always gets what he wants. And the mercenary wants Bethany in his bed. He wants her beautiful little body bent to his will.

She doesn't surrender to his kiss.

He doesn't back down from a challenge.

It's going to be a sensual fight… to the death.

Sign up for the VIP Reader List to find out when I have a new book release:
www.skyewarren.com/newsletter

Turn the page for an excerpt from Audition…

Excerpt from Audition

Bethany

BLINDING LIGHTS. ACHING lungs. Thunderous applause.

The opening show ends the way we rehearsed for weeks, only this time with an audience. My muscles know the movements better than they understand the rest. The prospect of after, of anything outside this stage, makes my breath catch.

We take our bows together, as a single line. The avant-garde dance company doesn't have a strict hierarchy—no corps dancers or prima ballerinas. There's only this show, this moment, which suits me perfectly. No promises. No regrets.

The curtain falls.

Almost to the second, we break formation—a flock of crows startled from the woods. We prance to the dressing room, our bodies made springy by adrenaline. Euphoria clings to our sweat-dampened skin even backstage.

Grins and congratulations all around.

The show is titled Olivia Twist, a contemporary retelling with most of the roles gender reversed. Fagin has been reimagined as Fanny, the clever head of a group home for girls. The concept was mine, but the entire show is a team effort.

There's relief, too. The standard ritual of icing swollen joints or wrapping bruised tendons. We hurl our bodies through the air, forcing massive impact through tired joints night after night. We look strong on stage. Behind the curtain we're a jumble of never-healing wounds, held together by silk and spandex and Kinesio tape.

I catch my friend Marlena under my shoulder. Her face is white with pain.

"Ice," she says. "Or better yet—tequila."

I push my shoulder under hers as we exit the stage. "Don't sell yourself short. You can have both."

A delicate snort. "Not likely. We have to smile and flirt with the old men with big, fat wallets. As if I don't do enough of that at home."

We fall into our creaky chairs in the dressing room. The stage director tosses half-frozen bottles of Ozarka at each of us, and we both pause to gulp. I'm wearing an army-green leotard sewn with rags to highlight my part as the gender-reversed Olivia Twist, while Marlena wears a patchwork greatcoat for her part as Fagin.

I drip some of the cold water into my palm and smooth it across the back of my neck. "You don't have to. At home, I mean. You definitely have to flirt at the opening party."

"My body hurts too much to give up my whirlpool tub or two thousand thread count sheets." Marlena has a sugar daddy who visits her a few times a week for an uncomplicated evening. In exchange he pays for an upscale brownstone once owned by a Hollywood actor, a Bentley and driver to take her to and from practice, and a 401K through his company.

"Does he have any friends?" I ask, though I'm joking—mostly.

"You know I'd find you a sugar daddy, if I thought you'd actually accept it. We probably don't even need to. I've seen the way Scott looks at your ass. He has more than enough money to keep both of us."

I choke on a swallow of water. "Marlena."

She giggles. "He may be old, but he knows how to show a girl a good time."

"We'll call that plan B. Besides, I like my apartment." The dance company doesn't pay very much. Less than minimum wage. They get away with it because it's considered a part-time job. We're only paid for the time we perform, even though we practice eight hours a day.

I don't precisely like my apartment, but it's all I can afford.

Marlena rolls her eyes. "Let me know when you get tired of the rat droppings."

For that comment I flick my fingers, spraying her with ice-cold water. She squeals and spills some of her water on my thigh, making me gasp. She thinks I'm too uptight to accept a sugar daddy, like maybe I look down on her. That's not it. I learned early on the risk of belonging to a man. The danger.

Being a ballet dancer is a terrible business model. My only commodity is my body, and between injury and age, it depreciates quickly. Still, it's managed to keep me off the streets. It's managed to keep me independent from my brother.

For that I'm grateful.

I remind myself of that as I sit at my bench. We're contractually obligated to attend the ball. Like Marlena said, we should smile and flirt with the rich people who attend. Both the male and female dancers have to. It's what convinces the sponsors to write checks that will fund the next season. Ticket sales don't even cover our tiny paychecks.

Fresh lipstick. Powder. I smooth a hand over my bun, but it's perfectly tight. The truth is that I look composed most of the time. People assume I must feel that way, too. It's an act as surely as I dance on the stage each night. A performance.

I'd love to change into a fresh leotard and shoes, but Rio would complain. They like us sweaty, the stage manager says. It adds to the authenticity. Five hundred rich people of New Orleans will be wearing gowns and tuxedos. Meanwhile I'm damp with sweat and the remains of our impromptu bottled water fight, wearing an army green leotard with bits of frayed fabric forming a ragged tutu.

Chandeliers blind me. The chatter is a physical sensation, like hitting a wall.

Rio hands me two glasses of champagne. "Dunn's on stage left."

My stomach sinks. Trevor Dunn is a real estate mogul who thinks his corporate sponsorship gives him the right to grope the dancers. Unfortunately he has a particular liking for me. I look around for Marlena, but she's already with Scott Castle. He stands in a black suit and silver-blond hair, a stern expression on his face. They met at one of these events last season, and he hasn't missed one since. He wants the other men to know she's taken. His hand on her ass doesn't leave any ambiguity.

From all the way across the room I hear Trevor's over-hearty laugh. God. He probably wants to become my sugar daddy. The idea makes my throat clench. My eyes burn.

Mamere's voice rumbles through my head. *You come from priestesses and warriors, child. Why you want to take off your clothes and dance for white men?* She's never thought ballet was different from being a stripper. As I approach the drunk men on the left side of the ballroom, the knot in my stomach tightening with every step, it feels like she's right.

It might seem like being on stage, but for me it's completely different. When I perform, my footwork is predetermined, the choreography practiced so well it feels like second nature. This? I try to avoid the boisterous crowd. People jostle me. They bump into me.

They make the champagne slosh against the glasses.

Golden liquid slips over the rim. It spills between my fingers. When I arrive at the group of men, they're caught in the grip of belly laughs—most likely over something lewd or offensive. These are the quintessential frat boys all grown up.

I'm the girl from a family where no one's been to college.

"Bethany," Trevor says with what I suppose is a charming smile on his perfectly tan face. He's aggressively fit, the kind that must take hours in a gym every morning. He's also aggressively styled with slick hair and expensive clothes and a gleaming male manicure. "You looked great tonight. I can pick you out of the lineup every time."

Heat rushes my face. He can pick me out of a *lineup* because of my skin color. It's not really a commentary on my talent or his skills of observation. "I brought champagne."

Only as the words leave my lips do I realize how strange it is for me to bring a glass only for him when he's standing in a group of other men. It's something a girlfriend would do.

I don't want him to get romantic ideas about me.

"Thanks, sweetheart." He hands me his empty beer stein, as if I'm a server.

It would be less humiliating if I weren't half-naked. The leotard which feels so natural onstage seems obscene as I stand here holding a glass smudged with Trevor Dunn's fingerprints.

I'm the high-society equivalent of a Hooter's waitress.

"That must be for me," comes a low voice I remember from my dreams. Green eyes. A face so handsome it belongs on some kind of movie star, not a soldier for hire. A mercenary. He wears his muscles with an ease that Trevor can't match. Those hands have done things that would make society matrons gasp. That body has moved through the darkest places on earth.

"You." My mind supplies only that word: you, you, you.

He gives me a cocky half smile that promises a wicked night. It's the smile that could lure Eve out of the garden. He's not Adam. No. He's the serpent with the dark temptation. "Hello, Bethany."

Trevor frowns. "You know her?"

"We've met," Josh says, taking the other champagne glass from my numb fingers. He takes a gulp before passing the flute to Trevor. He takes the beer stein, too, putting it in the crook of Trevor's suited elbow. That's how he leaves Dunn, holding three glasses, unable to move his arms without spilling. "Be a good pal and walk that over to the bar," Josh says, not taking his eyes off me.

It seems impossible that Trevor would obey. He does. His friends drift away, too.

Then it's only Joshua North standing in front of me.

"Why were you bringing that fucker a drink?"

His harsh tone makes me flinch. Which annoys me. I don't answer to this man. "It's not any of your business who I bring drinks to. What are you doing here?"

"I'm a fan of ballet," he says, his voice bland.

An unladylike snort. "Of course you are."

"What's not to like? Half-naked women on stage for an hour and a half. Doing the splits. Bending over. And those lifts. I swear your partner had his hand right in your—"

"Oh my God, you're worse than Trevor."

"That's his name?"

"You were talking to him."

"Only because I didn't know his name was Trevor."

My eyes narrow. "Why *are* you here again?"

"To see you, my darling, my love, my northern star."

He's making fun of me, which would be bad

enough—worse because my heart skips a beat at the words, eternally hopeful, eternally stupid. Once upon a time I had a crush on this man, even knowing he could never return the favor. The whole world is a joke to him. A dirty joke. "Fine, don't tell me."

"I could only count the days that we were apart. Desolate. Lonely."

He really is worse than Trevor. At least with Dunn I can slap away his grasping hands. When I get home it's easy enough to take a shower. Somehow I don't think hot water is going to wash away the sting of Joshua's mocking tone. "Whatever you're doing here, leave me out of it."

"That's going to be tough to do, sweetheart."

"Why's that?"

"Because I'm here to protect you."

Want to read more? Audition is available on Amazon, iBooks, Barnes & Noble, and other book retailers!

BOOKS BY SKYE WARREN

Endgame trilogy & Masterpiece Duet
The Pawn
The Knight
The Castle
The King
The Queen

Trust Fund Duet
Survival of the Richest
The Evolution of Man

Underground series
Rough
Hard
Fierce
Wild
Dirty
Secret
Sweet
Deep

Stripped series
Tough Love
Love the Way You Lie
Better When It Hurts
Even Better
Pretty When You Cry
Caught for Christmas
Hold You Against Me
To the Ends of the Earth

Standalone Books
Wanderlust
On the Way Home
Beauty and the Beast
Anti Hero
Escort

**For a complete listing of Skye Warren books,
visit**

www.skyewarren.com/books

About the Author

Skye Warren is the New York Times bestselling author of dangerous romance such as the Endgame trilogy. Her books have been featured in Jezebel, Buzzfeed, USA Today Happily Ever After, Glamour, and Elle Magazine. She makes her home in Texas with her loving family, sweet dogs, and evil cat.

Sign up for Skye's newsletter:
www.skyewarren.com/newsletter

Like Skye Warren on Facebook:
facebook.com/skyewarren

Join Skye Warren's Dark Room reader group:
skyewarren.com/darkroom

Follow Skye Warren on Instagram:
instagram.com/skyewarrenbooks

Visit Skye's website for her current booklist:
www.skyewarren.com/books

Copyright